THE DRAGON'S WORD

PERIDOT DRAGON SHIFTER BROTHERS

MARIE JOHNSTON

LE PUBLISHING

Editing and proofing by My Brother's Editor

Proofing by Deaton Author Services

Cover Art by Mayhem Cover Creations

Created with Vellum

Levi

I roll into town, planning to only meet the cat shifter female my family wants me to mate, when I witness a lovely vision walking across the street. That same beauty, with hair of spun gold, is challenged by a male in the parking lot. He wants her as his own, to dominate, to destroy. But there's one problem. She happens to be the girl I'm supposed to meet. So I stake my claim.

Briony

All I wanted to do was lie low. I'm a target for people who want to get to my pack leader grandmother. But when I'm challenged, another male steps in and says he's supposed to be my mate. He's a dragon shifter, and he's devastatingly handsome. It's hard to say no, but all he has to offer me is the same as what I have. Isolation and violence. No thanks. But Levi's determined to show me how sizzling being alone with him can be.

CHAPTER 1

riony

My grandmother was a scrappy female, full of piss and vinegar, ready to fight if someone said the word *go*. She was also opinionated and infuriating—especially when it came to me.

Most days I appreciated her ride-or-die attitude. Who else can say their gran has their back? Today was different. Today, she claimed to fight for my future but all she was doing was trying to pin me into a meaningless bond. All because I wanted everyone to mind their own business.

Shifters were not the people to tell to butt out.

"I don't think it's a good idea, Gran." I had only told her that once a day for the last two months.

"I think it's necessary, Briony."

I shook my head, my shoulder-length hair swinging. A lot of other females liked growing out their hair. For our kind, it was like a status symbol, just another way to show

how vibrantly healthy mountain lion shifters could be in their prime. Long hair, long legs, and a heightened sex drive.

The sex drive was harder to keep under control, but I couldn't be bothered with maintaining long locks. One time cleaning out the sink with my dad had been enough. I had to chop it that night, much to Gran's dismay, and never looked back. My dad hadn't said anything, but of course he wouldn't. After my mother had been killed, he'd indulged me. Whether it was easier to give in than to think about how my mom would've handled the situation, or because he would've been that way without my mom's stern resolve to balance him, I didn't know. And I hadn't cared. I had been going through my own grieving process and processing my own trauma. Not well, apparently, or I wouldn't be having this conversation with Gran.

My hair was just one of the ways I went against the stereotypical personality traits of my kind. Mountain lion shifters, or cat shifters as we preferred to say, were a lot of things I tried not to be. Quick to fight, indiscriminate in bed, and emotional rather than rational.

And I was struggling not to devolve into the stereotypical cat shifter. "I'm not mating him."

"He's a nice boy."

The "boy" in question was five years older than me. He was the youngest sibling in the Peridot clan, one of the dragon shifter clans across the Canada-US border. Peridot was in Minnesota. Except Levi had gone to North Dakota a few months ago. If I were to buy the story my gran told me, he was being mentored by the ruler of Jade clan. Levi Peridot had been traveling from clan to clan, getting to know all the rulers and, from what I'd heard, sample the females from each clan.

A typical young male dragon shifter. I didn't have to

meet him to know he thought he was all that and a bag of diamonds—and since he was a dragon shifter, he probably did have a bag of diamonds.

"You've never met him." I gave Gran my sternest stare.

She lifted her chin. "I am the leader of the pack. It's my job to know all the shifters in power, and Levi is one of the good ones." She matched my determined gaze. "And he's single. A single dragon shifter from a ruling family."

The dragon shifter part was the critical aspect of this whole situation. Gran was the leader of our pack, and she'd had to fight to maintain her position. My uncle Lewis was next in line, and no one messed with him. Naturally grumpy, he rose to a challenge quickly. Shifters had to be serious if they messed with him. Lewis was why Gran kept getting challenged, even in her seventies. People who wanted to overthrow her knew they wouldn't be able to take Uncle Lewis.

But over the years, they had realized I was Gran's weakness. My mother passed away when I was thirteen, and Gran had doted on me. She missed her daughter, I missed my mom, and we had bonded closer than ever before.

Those same people had also noticed I wasn't like Gran or my mom. I preferred books over beer, a nice walk over a sparring session, and a night full of laughter and chatting than frenzied fucking. Perhaps things would've been different if I hadn't gone through what I had when Mom was killed, but I had. And Dad and I had dealt with it ourselves, thinking we were sparing everyone trouble. I had hoped it worked, but Gran's recent trouble had been because of me.

I wanted to be left alone, and I did what I could to avoid confrontation. Very unshifterlike. I was tired of putting up with egos and attitudes. Others interpreted my behavior as a sign of weakness, but I didn't care.

Gran, however, did. Instead of fielding challenges as they came, she was the one issuing them when she heard disparaging comments about me. The last fight she had gotten in had taken her a full day longer to recover from than before. She was getting older. Eventually, she wouldn't be the victor. I couldn't let that happen. I'd lose her, and then Uncle Lewis would jump in to challenge whoever usurped her, killing that person. I'd lose more family.

Too much death.

I was over it, but I couldn't leave. Gran would continue to jump to my defense. Yet since I'd come home after finishing college, my presence had brought trouble. I wanted to move somewhere else in the world, a place far away from shifters. First, I had to know when the best time to leave was—and what I'd do with myself when I got there. I wasn't a dragon shifter with a hoard of jewels.

"You already know how I feel about mating Levi Peridot." Cat shifters didn't do arranged mating, and even if they did, the couple often met first.

But Gran wouldn't drop her stance. I just had to wait her out. Once Levi crossed my path, he'd lose any willingness to stick with me. I didn't do open relationships like some dragon shifters did, and I wasn't the usual type of playboy males. I covered as much skin as I showed, I didn't throw myself at males, and I'd rather not fight for my guy—a turnoff to a lot of shifters. Unlike the females who likely flocked his way, I wouldn't be stricken with mindless infatuation. I didn't covet power; therefore, his position as one of the ruling family didn't tempt me. We were probably as opposite as two people could be.

The matter should be settled before it had started, but

Gran was relentless. I did what I normally did when she brought Levi up and refused to change the subject. I found somewhere else to be.

"Do you want anything from the store? I'm going to grab some milk and eggs."

I hadn't baked as much in my life as I had staying with Gran. She had a sweet tooth a mile long, and I happened to love baking. It was something I had done with my mom. She had learned it from my gramps, but he had succumbed to injuries from a car accident years before I was born. My baking was probably nostalgic for Gran, but she'd never confess. So I made goodies, and she ate them.

Interest infused her expression. "What are you making next?"

"I found a recipe for chocolate cherry bars. Oh, I have to see if there's any baking chocolate left."

Gran lifted a bony shoulder. "There's not. I had a craving one night."

"That stuff is really bitter."

"So am I."

With a chuckle, I grabbed my purse and hooked it over my neck so it hung off the opposite hip and went out the door.

I wasn't worried about walking freely through Cougarton. I wasn't in a direct line for pack leadership, and that gave me a huge buffer of safety. In the year I'd been home from college and staying with Gran, people had made comments. They'd become increasingly insulting, but they hadn't been challenges. Gran was likely hoping to head off any outright confrontations by challenging first, but I didn't think anyone was serious. I didn't have anything to offer. I was an aimless college grad living with her grandmother in a small town.

Still, awareness prickled over the back of my neck and

down my spine. Surreptitiously, I glanced around as I covered the six blocks to the grocery store. Cars drove up and down the street, but the drivers paid me no mind. A couple was walking in the opposite direction on the other side of the street, and the path in front of me was wide open.

Was it my imagination? Was the talk of mating and super handsome Peridot shifters leaving me unsettled? Had others heard? Would it cause problems? Mating me would get someone closer to power. Uncle Lewis might be formidable but he wasn't indestructible. My cousin wasn't yet eighteen, and anyone who mated me would only have Uncle Lewis as a real opponent.

I glanced over my shoulder. Was I being watched? Studied?

A warm tremor traced over my skin, not the usual skin prickling. The image of Levi Peridot flashed through my mind. I shook my head. The more Gran talked about him, the more often I looked him up. Hearing his name over the years with less than mild interest about the details was a different beast than seeing pictures. And there was a lot of him grinning in selfies and at parties. Several with humans, all in Minneapolis. One was him at a beach, some lake in Minnesota, and he had his shirt off.

It was unfair that he knew how sexy he was.

Levi had a permanently tanned complexion thanks to his Métis ancestors, inky-black hair that he kept long enough on the top to pull into a ponytail in the back over his shaved sides. And then I'd seen a picture of him without his hair secured. The way it flopped over his forehead and gave his sharp green-yellow eyes a mysterious edge wasn't fair. Some people were born with all the gifts. If he was smart too, I would hate him on principle.

I feathered my fingers through my mousy-brown hair. Gran called it golden, but I called the shade common. Basic. Like me.

I swept through the store quick enough, the edge of my nerves sharpening further. I wanted to return home and lose myself in grating the new bar of dark chocolate I had just bought. Being in the kitchen was soothing. I didn't do much to release the natural aggression shifters had, but cooking and baking helped. I wished I had more people to make food for.

A shiver scraped down my spine as soon as I swept out the door of the grocery store. A rough-looking man reclined against a big red pickup parked in the disabled parking spot. DJ was not disabled, but the monstrosity he was leaning against was his. He'd been showing up where I'd been running errands lately. Gran had muttered his name the other day, but when I'd asked her what he'd done, she'd brushed me off.

DJ was older than me, and I'd never liked him. He'd leered at me, but he'd never made a move. I'd come home to visit during college and it'd be the same creepy, territorial stare, but that was all. I thought I was safe from more than his mere presence.

I veered to the right. Best wishes to whatever girl he was waiting for.

He tracked me, his gaze like a splash of tepid grease on my skin. "Briony."

I didn't stop. I had nothing to say to the male. He was slimy, and he looked at me like he'd already stripped my clothes off and violated me. The company he kept was almost as bad.

"You're going to want to stop for this," he said, his tone taunting.

It was the smug gotcha element in his voice that made

me stop. At least he was alone. I turned around, ignoring the slam of a car door to my right. In times like this, I got tunnel vision. I didn't want to notice all the witnesses. I was a cat shifter. I was expected to help myself.

Too bad I'd seen the outcome. I lived with the consequences. No one here knew how ugly our true nature could get and if they did and didn't care, then I wanted to be far away from them.

But then I'd remember Gran lying broken in her bed, struggling to stay alive long enough for her body to have a chance to heal itself. She'd done that for me. And the way Dad had been devastated after Mom's death. How he'd shut down and isolated himself on the farm. I didn't want to be that responsibility for anyone. I was on my own.

"Why do you say that?" I asked. DJ was a lot of things, but he didn't make false boasts. If he told a female he was going to fuck her up, he meant it, and not in a good way from the rumors I'd heard.

His sneer made my insides curl into a ball and ping-pong around my abdominal cavity looking for a dark corner to hide in. "Because..." His smile stretched wider, like he was going to gobble me up—again, not in a good way. "I'm challenging you."

My stomach bottomed out. Crap. I'd never been officially challenged. Dad had trained me how to fight, and I was confident I could take care of myself, but I hadn't imagined having to fight a male like DJ. He had the size and strength to back up his cruelty, and death would be the preferable outcome. If he won, he'd claim me.

I shuddered. No thank you. I couldn't risk it.

I'd have to use my brains to get out of this. First, I needed facts. "Why would you want to challenge me?"

"Because you're mine." And his lips spread wider, revealing long canines for a human.

I had the incredible urge to drop to my knees and retch. Mate DJ? The experience would be awful. It'd be demeaning. There would be no pleasure for me, and he'd get more delight out of my pain. I'd heard the stories of the females he was with. I'd been his weird little obsession since we were kids. As an adult, I didn't want to experience firsthand what he would do to me.

When you don't know the answer, repeat the question. It wasn't the best advice, but it would buy me a few seconds while I tried to figure my way out of this treacherous maze. "You want to challenge me in order to mate me?"

"You're already mine. You just don't know it yet. I allowed you to go out and have your fun, get that useless college degree, but now you're back where you belong, and that's with me."

He allowed? I swallowed a gag. "Why didn't you try, I don't know, asking me out?"

He moved his tongue like he was flipping a toothpick from one side to the other, as if he was some 1950s thug. "Where's the fun in that?"

I wrinkled my nose, showing my disgust, not caring how it came across to him or the others watching. "I really hope you're not one of those guys that get off on violence. It's *really* unsexy."

There was a snicker off to my left and DJ's gaze sharpened, zeroing in on me, rage blowing his pupils open. "You're going to find out what gets me off."

This wasn't going well but the cat in me couldn't tip my tail and smile pretty. I adopted a bored demeanor, hoping he was too upset to hear my heart racing. "So, about this challenge... I have a headache tonight. And I wanted to bake some bars for Gran. Tomorrow, I have some errands to run. Where am I supposed to fit you in?"

I might as well go to the hardware store across the

street and buy myself a shovel because I was digging my own grave.

DJ pushed off the pickup and prowled toward me. I took a step back, terrified but willing to let him think I wouldn't fight. I would, but I'd rather make him overconfident first.

"You're not going to make it back to your little old gran, Briony. We're doing this now."

Oh shit, oh shit, oh shit. What was I going to do?

"That's not going to happen," a rich, deep voice that practically petted my nerves into submission said.

DJ jerked his head to my right. I couldn't bring myself to look. The voice wasn't familiar and I could be imagining the male coming to my rescue. Or maybe he just wanted a quiet shopping trip and would ask DJ to take the challenge elsewhere.

"Stay the hell out of this," DJ sneered, his hands curling into fists.

We weren't allowed to shift in public, but that wouldn't stop DJ from starting a fight in his human form. Cat shifters lived in the same communities their packs did, but many humans also resided in the same places.

"You dragged me into this," the delicious voice said. "As soon as you challenged my mate."

That got me to swing my head around and find out who was speaking. My gaze landed on the male from my dreams, the guy I'd been low-key obsessing over and insisting to Gran I wasn't interested in, Levi Peridot.

Wait—had he just called me his mate?

~

Levi

. . .

When I rolled into Cougarton, I expected to drive around town and get to know the layout before I pulled up in front of Enid Croft's place and talked to her about her granddaughter Briony. I'd let her down gently without affecting relations between border pack and dragon shifters. That was the plan.

Then I'd seen a shot of spun gold crossing the street. My dragon eye couldn't resist seeing who had hair that looked like I could take her in to find out how much I'd get for a lock.

I told myself I was crazy when I turned my car around to follow her into the grocery store parking lot. She'd been looking around like she was worried she was being followed, yet she was oblivious to me. The air of paranoia around her could have been created in her mind, or maybe it was real. I had been compelled to follow her and make sure she was okay.

It had nothing to do with watching the way her tits bounced underneath her pink tank top as she walked or how bronzed her skin looked against the yellow fabric of her shorts. She looked like a damn flower bebopping across the road.

After I had parked, I watched her disappear into the store, and then that asshole showed up. I hadn't liked his demeanor or the coincidental way he arrived when she had. My concern increased when he hadn't gone into the store. Instead he leaned across the hood and waited and I couldn't escape the idea that we were waiting for the same girl.

The confrontation had happened, and my concerns had been validated. But they left me in a pickle. As soon as the douchebag had said her name, I knew today wasn't about coincidences. The female I'd been watching was Briony Sanders. The female I was told I should mate. It'd be a symbiotic relationship. She could help me get back in the good graces of my clan's council members, and my sister, the ruler of the clan. Briony would be protected as my mate. Jackasses like the one who challenged her would leave her alone.

And unfortunately, the only way I could think to help her was to announce I was her mate when I wasn't even her promised mate. No one had to know we hadn't met. As long as she played along.

She had to. There was no way she'd allow this guy's filthy fingers on her.

The male who challenged her squared his shoulders and prowled closer to her as he watched me. "What the fuck did you just say?"

I took a chance and glanced at the female I had come to meet. Her plump lips had fallen open and her eyes were wide. Damn, but she had a ripe mouth. What was she thinking?

I knew next to nothing about her. From what I'd heard, I'd gotten the impression I would come to town and find an entitled, spoiled brat. A female who'd grown up under the protection of her family, who didn't think she had to work for what she had, including defending herself. Her grandmother had been in several fights because of her, and that didn't sit right with me.

But seeing Briony was changing the image I'd had. On the outside, she looked meek. I wouldn't be surprised if she played up that side of her personality in order to throw others off. Was her grandmother a firecracker, impulsively smacking down anyone she thought would endanger her granddaughter?

The way Briony turned the argument on DJ, stripping him down and insulting him while almost ignoring the gravity of his demands was unexpected. She wasn't meek, and she was crafty.

However, she was still a petite female. If she could fight like most shifters knew how to, I doubted she could compare to DJ's much larger size and sheer cruelness. The vibes emanating off of him left a sour taste in my mouth. The zeal in his eyes when he talked about forcing her to his submission put my teeth on edge.

No. There would be no challenge. I would plant myself firmly between them.

Briony snapped her mouth shut and blinked. "Levi?"

I inclined my head, certain I had the right female and there wasn't more than one Briony walking around the small border town of the tongue in cheek named Cougarton. What a way for us to meet.

"Nice to see you," was all I said, and her eyes flared further.

DJ tracked our interaction. "The fuck you two are getting mated."

I looked down on him. He was a big guy with bulkier muscles than me, but I had an inch of height on him. "I wasn't aware I needed your approval, cat."

Her lip curled up in the corner. Yeah, I wasn't below the subtle pointing out that I was both a dragon shifter and from a ruling family.

Turning my attention back to Briony, the dragon inside me loved how flecks of yellow scattered in the amber of her eyes. I had a fondness for brown emeralds and her eyes reminded me of the favorite jewels of my hoard.

The male interrupted my perusal. "Who the fuck are you anyway?" He stepped closer and lowered his voice. "You're a dragon shifter. There's no damn way you're mating *her*." The disdain that dripped from the word "her" told me everything I needed to know about this male. He didn't respect Briony; he wanted to conquer her. His reason could be just because, or because she was the granddaughter of their pack leader. Briony had power and a protective circle he hadn't been able to breach. A guy like him didn't tolerate that kind of stuff well.

"Talk about her that way again and I'll rip you apart," I said evenly. My bold statement was just shy of a promise, one I'd be glad to be held to. Dragons didn't make promises easily. Failing to carry out our word could mean death.

Anger flashed across his face and he puffed his chest out. I'd heard the other types of shifters could partially shift without turning entirely into their beast. Little enhancements they couldn't maintain long. Longer canines or bigger muscles. Ultimately, it was nothing more than a parlor trick and behavior that endangered the secret of their kind.

Ignoring him, I turned toward Briony. "I can give you a ride home."

She peered at me like I was a specimen under a microscope. I could honestly say no female had looked at me the way she had. My ego almost withered. Had I thought I'd swoop in, declare myself her mate, and she'd throw herself into my arms?

Maybe a little.

"How did you…" She shook her head, her gaze darting to DJ. "Yeah, I'd appreciate it."

The lilt of her voice washed over me until the sound was imprinted in my eardrums. This female was mine, but from the set of her flat lips, I was the only one who thought so.

What was her issue? Why was her grandmother fighting her battles? And if she didn't like Enid standing up for her, then why didn't she like the idea of mating with me?

I walked Briony to the passenger door of my black Lexus. My dragon shifter status gave me another buffer DJ would hate. Challenges among our kind were done in our animal form, and it was hard for a mountain lion to take on a dragon. Not impossible, but often a little more of a nuisance for a dragon to take on another kind of shifter.

I opened the door for her and she slid in, her cinnamon-sugar scent caressing my olfactory nerves. That couldn't be her real smell. Perhaps the bags of groceries she settled between her feet were full of goodies. My stomach clenched, reminding me I had driven through lunch. But when I thought of eating, it wasn't food spread out in front of me.

Dammit, I had to get control of myself. My thoughts and assumptions had been stirred into a frenzy and tossed out on the hot pavement. I had to gather myself and find out what was going on, especially since I'd just announced in public that the female sitting in my car, whom I barely knew, would be my mate.

CHAPTER 2

riony

COULD he hear how hard my heart was hammering? I licked my lips, hoping to add some moisture to my dry mouth before he got into the car. In seconds, I would be closed into the cab with Levi Peridot. I never thought I would cross paths with him, much less witness him announce in front of the occupants of Teller's grocery store I was his promised mate.

He got behind the wheel, and I took a deep breath, instantly regretting the decision. A rich amber scent with notes of dark chocolate surrounded me. He could *not* smell that good, but I didn't detect the chemical undertones of cologne or aftershave. I wouldn't be able to make any chocolate baked goods now without thinking of him.

He didn't say a word as he pulled out of his parking space, giving the people watching us a good-natured wave.

I couldn't even summon a fake smile. As he turned out of the parking lot, the sense that I was being led to a walled prison weighed on me.

"You don't have to mate me," I blurted.

He didn't spare me a glance, but his fist tightened around the wheel, and I was captivated by the flexing muscles in his forearms. A guy shouldn't make charcoal slacks and a white button-up shirt look so good. It should also be illegal for him to roll up the sleeves of that shirt.

I'd never been a superficial girl. A male's appearance only mattered in that he cared for himself. I didn't get all aquiver when a guy had his hair just right or possessed a trendy fashion sense. Classically handsome equals classically boring, in my opinion. I cared more about the brain in his head than the hardness of his body.

Or so I had thought. It seemed my preferences had been obliterated.

"Let me ask you this," he said, executing a turn that would bring us to Gran's in two blocks.

"How do you know where I live?" I asked, needing the answer before he asked his question.

This time he glanced at me out of the corner of his eye, and I was captivated. I'd noticed his eye color online when I first saw him. He was a hard male not to notice, and his unusually bright-green eyes made him stand out. But this close, they were fascinating. I had heard of dragon shifters and their jewel hoards, but it looked like he took two of his favorite gems and used them in place of his irises. An image that shouldn't work, but only completed the inhumanly sexy package of Levi Peridot.

"It's a small town, and I'm an inventive guy."

The way he said those words in the low rumble of his voice was like a direct connection to a libido I'd been beating back with a stick for years. A shiver ran through my body, but thankfully he'd already turned his attention back to the road.

When he parked, I didn't rush to get out. Once Gran saw he was in town, the fight for my personal freedom would become three times harder. "Seriously, why are you here?"

He inhaled slowly, then twisted to look at me, resting his elbow on the console. I pressed my back against the door in a failed attempt to create more space between us, but now that I'd met him, I didn't think there was a corner of the earth far away enough to hide from his magnetism.

"I don't know what you've heard," he said, "but a stupid oversight disrupted my entire life. And it sounds like you're in a similar boat." He lifted a shoulder and the cat in me noticed the way the fabric moved over his muscles. Smooth, sinuous moves did it for my inner kitty. "I don't know how much of it is your fault, or if you're like me, a victim of circumstance, but I'm trying to own my role in what happened, and that includes appeasing the council members of my clan to make my sister's job easier. But I am almost twenty-eight, and I'm going to have to settle down soon enough, so when your name was brought up, and I was told about the position you're in, I figured I might as well come and check the situation out."

The situation being me and how Gran was fighting my battles without asking me first. I digested what he said. Dragon shifters had to mate by the time they were thirty-five. The other types of shifters, like cat shifters, didn't have the same restrictions. Our natural aggression didn't grow unchecked without a stabilizing force. We were naturally more aggressive than humans, and in dragons, it was amplified more. It was up to the leaders of the pack or clan to maintain a vigilant code of behavior.

"What happened?" I needed to hear him explain why he'd been basically kicked out of his clan. I'd heard terms like he'd been told he had to grow up, or that his council wanted him terminated and the other dragon clan rulers were helping protect him. None of it made sense. Dragon shifters didn't sleep on termination orders. They were efficient but ruthless, no matter how hard the job was to carry out. There were too many repercussions in delay. Dragon shifters were too big, too noticeable, to indiscriminately get out of line and start fights.

"I was hanging out with a friend," he started.

"Brighton Garnet." She was mated now, but had she been seeing Levi? Why was envy burning in my chest?

He dipped his head. "She was trying to live a little before deciding whether Ronan Jade was the right male for her." He slid his gaze toward me. "That part stays between us."

"It's not as juicy as any of the rumors I heard, so no one will care anyway." Ruling families and who they were mating were shifters' versions of Gran's soap operas. "The talk included you."

The angles of his face hardened and irritation momentarily brightened his eyes. Was he upset about the rumors about him or Brighton, or both? "There was a guy, a human, who took an interest in her, but she stood up to him. Creeps like that don't take getting put in their place by what they think is a little woman in stride. He knew we hung out, so he followed me, trying to find her." He gave his head a little shake. "I should've been paying attention. But I had a lot on my mind, and I just wanted to take flight and clear my head. He was good enough to follow me without being noticed—clearly had experience with stalking women—and he saw me shift."

"Oh, no," I breathed.

A muscle in the corner of his jaw jumped. "He thought he'd use it as leverage to find Brighton. He tried blackmailing me, and he learned my sister is the mayor of Peridot Falls, so he took his threats to her. And she killed him. The council was understandably upset."

To outsiders, the rulers of dragon shifter clans were mayors. Everything on the books looked like they got elected when they were actually born into rule. I could see the internet search that led the human straight to Memphis's door and his death. I could also see how Levi shouldered the blame, and why his tight-knit clan was unsettled. He'd led a human right to their door. Shifted in front of him. A mistake like that could get any of us killed.

He met my gaze and I forgot to breathe. His eyes were stunning and when they were on me, my mind didn't want to work. "Your turn. What's your story?"

My story was being born in the wrong life. "Gran grew up in a different world than I did. Instead of using words, she uses claws. She thinks she is preventing trouble. When I refuse to start a fight unless I'm directly challenged, I'd later find out she'd issued a challenge herself and fought the person who insulted me." Looking toward Gran's house, I broke the connection between us. Having Levi Peridot's full attention on me was disconcerting. I was used to being overlooked and ignored. If I wasn't Enid's granddaughter, I'd be invisible. "I didn't know about the first two fights until later. But the last time, she almost didn't make it. I can handle myself, but most of the time I don't feel the need to. After what happened to my mom… she's terrified to lose me too."

"You didn't know your gran was fighting on your behalf?" He sounded perplexed, disbelieving.

"Do you think I'd lie about something like that?" I

didn't need some entitled guy from a ruling family questioning my integrity. Gran was all I had. I grabbed the door handle and pulled but the door was locked. Flustered, I started punching at buttons. The window went down, then back up, then I hit the lock button, and finally unlock. I pushed the door open. "You don't know me. And that's why you shouldn't have bothered coming."

I scrambled to get out of the car, but before I could swing my legs out, a plastic grocery bag caught on my feet and ripped, the contents spilling on the floor of his car. This was just getting better and better.

A deep vibration gave me pause. Was he laughing? I jerked my head toward him only to be entranced by a wide smile with sharp canines that made my kitty purr.

"It isn't funny," I mumbled. He didn't need to enhance himself like DJ.

"It sort of is."

I'd been laughed at enough in my life. People like Levi were the reason I didn't want anything to do with my own kind. I fumbled with all the groceries, attempting to get them back in part of the bag so I could use it like a pouch, but the tear just kept growing wider.

Levi got out of the vehicle. I thought he would walk straight to the front door, leaving me to clean up my own mess, which I'd be grateful for. A little humiliation in private beat a public spectacle any day.

But then he was squatting in the open doorway and gathering the dark chocolate bar, the vanilla, the brown sugar, and the five-pound bag of flour that had been the plastic bag's ultimate demise in his arms. The only thing he didn't grab was a carton of eggs. And dammit, I forgot milk.

I prided myself on being a big enough person to show

gratitude when it was deserved. But it still grated to say, "Thank you."

"Don't mention it. I got the door."

I crawled out, holding my dozen eggs, and he hip-checked the door shut. He lifted his chin in a *lead the way* gesture, and I tucked my bag close to my chest and headed toward the front door. Gran had probably seen the whole thing, and she'd only be encouraged.

I wasn't. Tonight, I would figure out a new time line for my life. The plan to move to a big city and lose myself in humanity was just moved up several years.

Gran was at the door by the time we reached the top step. Levi inclined his head. "Ma'am."

Her sharp gaze immediately softened. I knew the feeling. It was hard not to turn to putty around Levi. Didn't the rest of his clan feel this way? I couldn't imagine the gallant male I'd just met being driven out of his town.

"Levi Peridot. You didn't call when you got to town." Typical Gran. She wasn't completely won over by pretty looks and empty sayings, instead getting right down to the heart of the matter. Levi was from a ruling family of dragon shifters, and he was in town ultimately on business.

I was that business.

And since I was also the reason he hadn't stopped to call, I gently elbowed past him. "I'm surprised you haven't already heard, Gran. Come on in, Levi. You can set your armload on the counter."

Gran stepped back to let us inside. He was at least six inches taller than her and almost a foot taller than me. My mom had been between Gran and me for height, and my dad was almost six feet tall. I didn't know where my short genes came from, but they could be mighty inconvenient in the shifter world. It was like I was expected to be more of a wolverine with my diminutive height, like I needed a bigger attitude to make up for a lack of inches.

Gran and Levi crowded into the kitchen.

"I'll let Briony tell the story." Levi remained standing by the island, and Gran and I both stared at him for a moment.

Finally, Gran swept a hand toward the small square kitchen table on the other side of the room. "Please, have a seat. I assume you're here on friendly terms?"

"Depends on who you ask," he said with a touch of humor. "When it comes to you, yes. Friendly terms." His gaze landed on me and it was like the oven behind me was a raging fireplace. Heat blanketed me until it was hard to draw a breath.

I was used to attention from males, but the type I received in the past was a lot more like the confrontation with DJ today. I was something to be conquered, claimed. A prize that I was afraid would only get used up and trodden as my dominant partner moved on to something more exciting.

Sure, the female part of me got as excited as anyone else when I thought of a dominant male partner, but not like that. I wanted equality to be the basis of my relationship, a give-and-take. I hadn't met anyone who didn't seem to want to do more than take from me to prove something selfish inside themselves. As a kid, friends had tried to butter up to Gran. Guys who asked me out had their eye on pack leadership, like I was a stepping-stone. That burned by itself, but to imagine they'd fight my grandmother for a little extra power? Unconscionable.

What did Levi want? He was here, so he was either open to the idea of us, or I was just an excuse to keep the distance between him and his clan. He might not care about pack leadership, no dragon shifter would, but he cared about impressing his own leadership.

"What happened?" Gran asked just as her phone started vibrating.

Since whoever was calling her was likely going to gleefully report everything that had happened in the parking lot, I let the story rush out. "DJ challenged me, I insulted him, and then Levi showed up and claimed he's my mate."

I expected anger to turn her face red. Then I'd have to figure out a way to talk her into staying before she marched out of the house. The last two times I had been confronted by males who insinuated they wanted to fight me for the right to mate me, Gran had disappeared for hours. And then I'd learned she fought on my behalf.

But a smile lit her from inside out like she was a Christmas candle. "That'll work just fine." She pulled her phone out of the pocket of her gray slacks and practically danced out of the kitchen.

Levi kicked his feet out and crossed his arms. The house was old, and the kitchen was small with no separate dining room. He shouldn't fill the room like he did, but his presence was as undeniable as the rest of him.

Nerves made me fidgety, and there were only two things I liked to do when my anxiety ran rampant. Lose myself in my studies, or bake. Since I was out of school and I hadn't decided on a master's degree, I'd have to make those chocolate cherry bars I promised her.

"Will she confront DJ?" Levi asked.

I started pulling ingredients out of the refrigerator. "After that reaction? I doubt it." I spun, leaving the fridge door hanging open. "But if she says she has to go somewhere, I need to stop her because she's probably going to start some shit again."

"How do you mean?"

I kicked the door closed and grabbed the salt, cinnamon, and baking soda from the neighboring cupboard and swung the door shut. "Every time she's learned about stuff like that"—I jerked my head in the general direction of the grocery store—"she's vanished for a while, and then I learned she was issuing her own challenge."

"We're shifters, Briony. Situations don't get handled by talking."

They would if Levi was speaking. That low rumble? The way he held eye contact while he spoke like I was the only one in the room. Well, I was, but still. He was potent.

"We need to do better," I snapped.

He did nothing more than arch a dark brow. He put his feet flat on the floor and sat forward, leaning those sinful forearms on the tops of his thighs. A lock of his dark hair fell over his forehead, and I imagined a magazine photographer striding in for the perfect shot. The image of him in this moment was blazed into my brain.

"Do we?" he asked. When I stopped digging through a drawer looking for the measuring cups I'd need, he continued. "Maybe the real question is, why are you trying to be so human?"

"Humans didn't kill my mother." I went back to riffling through the drawer, but I couldn't focus on the measuring sizes, my vision growing blurry. I refused to cry.

He moved so quickly and silently, I jumped when he appeared next to me. Wrapping his big, warm hand around my wrist until I stopped creating the clattering noise filling the kitchen, he dipped his head down. "I'm sorry."

I blinked rapidly, chasing away any rogue tears that had gathered in my eyes. "You didn't know. The point is, fighting does no good. It steals people from loved ones when a stern conversation would've done the trick."

"We can't change our nature." He released my hand slowly, almost as if he didn't want to let me go. I mourned the loss of his touch and wondered when I'd get to experience it again.

"Oh, but we did." I didn't have to crane my head back as far as I thought to look up at him. The feel of his hand on my skin lingered, making it hard for me to form a sentence. "When our ancestors made the deal with the powers of the world at the time to walk in human form as shifters, they changed their nature." I poked his chest and it absolutely was not a reason just to touch him. My word, he had rock-solid pecs. "You're here now because your dragon ancestors wished to change their nature. You might be able to heal yourself just like the rest of us shifters, but you're not immortal anymore."

He tilted his head, his gaze not unkind, but interested, as if he liked the challenging conversation. Usually, by this point, I received disgusted looks or headshakes as people looked for the nearest exit. "They saw the writing on the cave—humans were taking over the earth. But I'm a dragon shifter, Briony. You're a mountain lion shifter."

"Cat shifter." At his quizzical look, I elaborated. "Why use four syllables when one does the trick?"

"Because when I hear you say cat shifter, I think of a spoiled tabby cat lying in a sunbeam."

I snorted. "Don't I wish."

His laugh kept me frozen in place. Deep and rich, it was as intoxicating as his appearance and his scent. Was there anything about this guy that wouldn't keep me riveted?

"Maybe we'll get there eventually." His gaze tracked my movements as I pulled out a recipe card and started measuring flour and sugar. "Give us some more time to evolve."

My answer was a mild grunt. Unprepared for the way he listened to me and contributed to the conversation instead of trying to stop it cold or humiliate me so I wouldn't bring up the topic again was unexpected. He was from a ruling family, yet he was more down to earth than the cat-shifter males who'd tried to date me.

I poured the sugar into a saucepan and unwrapped the chocolate bar.

"What are you making?" he asked.

For God's sake, he was even interested in my baking? How badly did I want to go my own way and get lost in the big city? If this male was willing to mate me, I should dive on his offer and jump on him as fast as I could.

The sight of my mom lying in a pool of blood, her throat slit so deep no shifter could heal from the wound, was branded in my mind. I couldn't end up with the same fate, and if my present was anything to judge my future by, I would share a similar end. He might be down to earth, but ruling families were ruling families and life was more dangerous for them. I was trying to get away from that.

I cleared the sudden thickness from my throat. "Chocolate cherry bars. I bake when I'm stressed." Why did I tack on the last part? He didn't need to know. My father would say telling a shifter your weakness was a poor strategy.

He leaned his hands on the counter, oblivious to the dusting of flour pressing into his slacks. "What are you stressed about?"

"You were there." I methodically chopped the chocolate bar, leaning into all the routine activities that usually steadied my mind.

"But you were buying the supplies before that guy challenged you."

Why couldn't he be an idiot? Did I tell him, or did I brush off his attempt at conversation like so many had done to me?

If I couldn't be honest with the male I didn't want to mate with for the rest of my life, then who could I be honest with? Lies would only lead him on—as if someone like me could lead a guy like him anywhere. But I had enough nontruths and secrets in my life.

"I have a plan for my life." The knife rhythmically thunked on the cutting board as I chopped the chocolate finer than was necessary. "And it's not staying in the shifter town where my freedom can get taken away while I'm running to the grocery store for milk and eggs."

"You didn't get milk."

"Thus introducing another problem in my life." Maybe I could pick up milk at the gas station. I wasn't ready to show my face in any business in town yet. People would stare; they might even ask questions. I didn't have answers and like another time in my life, the truth would cause more issues, get more people embroiled in violence. I'd been there before.

DJ couldn't know Levi was lying. Sort of. People wanted us to mate, but we weren't promised to each other.

"Where would you go? And I don't mean to get milk."

"I'm not a dragon shifter, so I can go anywhere."

I glanced up to catch his expression. Dragon shifters had to live in specifically dragon shifter communities. Typically, they lived with their own clan, but they could intermate and move to another clan as long as it was dragon shifters. Our packs weren't as tightly knit, but the creatures we shifted into weren't as large either. A human could freak over a mountain lion running through town, but a big cat was easier to explain. It was hard to justify why a dragon was flying around.

He didn't react to my statement, probably because it was his reality and he accepted it. "And where does anywhere include?"

"A big city. I want to get lost in anonymity. I want my only worry about guys to be annoying pickup lines at the bar. And since I don't go to the bars, and I don't get hit on unless a guy's interested in carving their way to being a pack leader, then I won't have to worry about that either."

I dumped the chopped chocolate into the saucepan and brushed all the dust in after it. Turning my back to Levi, I put the pan on the stove and measured the rest of the ingredients into it for the chocolate sauce.

He stayed where he was. "I used to go to Minneapolis all the time. It got my ass in trouble, but I can understand the draw of being lost in the crowd, of being just another one of the masses."

I grabbed a wooden spoon out of a holder that said *for stirrin' or for smackin'*. Gran's sense of humor that I hoped Levi didn't notice. "But you can see how there's conflict. Why I can't mate you and you don't want to mate me."

"I never said a thing about who I do or don't want to mate, but there's plenty of conflict."

I sensed Gran before she popped in the doorway. "I have the guest room all ready for you, Levi."

My stirring came to a halt. "He's staying here?"

Levi's gaze didn't pull away from me to answer Gran. "That's one problem taken care of. Thank you, Enid."

I looked between both of them. Levi's measured stare and Gran's triumphant expression. "Won't it give everyone the wrong idea?" More like it'd support everyone's assumption I was mating the Peridot sibling. Since he'd announced it.

Gran lifted a finely trimmed gray brow. "No, it'll make assholes like DJ back off. Levi is our guest, and I will treat him as such, but I'm not going to deny that he did us a giant favor and we owe him." Her tone said I would be the one paying up.

"But…" Gran's house was my sanctuary in Cougarton. I could be myself within these walls and roam without being worried about confrontation.

Gran held my gaze, quelling any argument. She was still my pack leader too, and not just my overprotective grandmother. "Keep stirring. I don't want charred chocolate in my bars."

"I'll go grab my things," Levi said. When he left the kitchen, Gran followed.

I was alone and I should be grateful, but… I enjoyed talking to him. A feeling I didn't often get.

I glowered at the slowly melting chocolate. I woke up a single female intent on keeping Gran out of trouble. Why did I feel like I was going to bed promised to a male who could only offer me everything I didn't want?

~

Levi

THE ROOM ENID led me to was up a steep flight of stairs at the back of the house. The room itself was actually an attic that had been converted to a bedroom. A window had been added on either side of the house, under the peak of the roof. The stairs crested in the middle of the room with a railing around the opening. There was no door. My first thought when I saw the opening in the floor was that I had one less thing between me and Briony.

Enid swept through the room, peering in each corner as if she'd personally mutilate any dust bunny she found. "I hope this is sufficient. I imagine your place in Peridot Falls is a lot nicer."

I lived on my own in the little house on the edge of town. Tucked deep into the woods where I could have all the privacy I wanted. Unless a deranged stalker followed me home and saw me shift. The only night I hadn't driven home first, and then marched into the woods. I had taken a more common back road and parked in an off-the-beaten-path area not many humans or shifters knew about. A place dark enough, isolated enough, that the man who had wanted to hurt my friend could park far enough away that I didn't sense him and watch me with a pair of night-vision binoculars.

The biggest mistake of my life. I had put my people at risk, and I wouldn't forgive myself. Memphis and Maverick had been upset, but they had forgiven me. Still didn't mean they took me seriously. Briony and I had that in common.

It was easy to see the root of her frustration. We were two shifters, searching for our place in our individual worlds. The only difference was that she could go anywhere. My place was Peridot Falls, which was fine with me. I just wanted something to do there other than bum around and be a nobody.

"This will be fine," I said. "I appreciate not having to find other accommodations, especially since I don't know who is pro DJ and against DJ."

She crossed her arms over her chest. "I imagine it changes depending on who you talk to. This pack is getting a serious case of waffling. Shifters who can't stand up for themselves are hiding behind those who are just plain mean. They have to learn to stand up for themselves instead of expecting me to fight all their battles."

"Are you including your granddaughter in that statement?" Was Briony's assessment correct, or had she been deluding herself about Enid to make herself feel better?

"Verbally? She can slaughter anyone within hearing distance. But physically?" Enid shook her head. "Her dad said he taught her to fight, but I haven't seen it. She's a damn pacifist. Ultimately, it doesn't matter. She might know how to spar, but males like DJ were born scrapping and only grew up crueler and more entitled as their strength won more fights than their brains. This whole pack feels like it's full of DJs most days."

"You're a formidable leader."

She nodded, pride shining over her features. "And my son will do just fine. He's even-keeled but tough like me. But he's not exactly like minded when it comes to Briony. He thinks she should prove herself and doesn't understand why she walks away."

"And you think that as long as her place isn't a leader, she should be left the hell alone?"

A steely glint flashed deep in her irises. "Exactly."

"I didn't have a chance to have a nice chat with DJ, but I don't think he's going to leave her alone." I narrowed my gaze on her. "And it won't do you or Briony any good to go charging after him."

Enid was tough, and she'd proven herself time and again. But there was a dangerous air about DJ that made me think of the stalker who'd zeroed in on Brighton. A little unstable, much too determined, and if he came out the victor, the entire pack would be in a world of hurt.

Enid sighed, the edge around her softening. "I know what you're saying. But you showing up at the same time he issued his challenge and saving us a heap of trouble? That's more than a coincidence. It's fate."

I couldn't deny I was drawn to Briony. I had found her alluring before she'd hooked me with her personality. Staying in Cougarton and getting to know her suited me just fine, but the added pressure of DJ turned a quick visit to check things out into forever. "I only just met her today. It'd be nice to have some time."

"Sure would be nice," Enid said as if the complications with what happened today was obvious. And they were. Briony wanted to get lost in the big city. She wanted freedom, and life in a dragon shifter clan would be the opposite. She'd be under higher scrutiny because she was my mate, and everyone would know who she was. I was the ruler's brother, and my mate's actions would be monitored and commented on.

Peridot Falls was the opposite of a big city with its one main street, a few scattered neighborhoods, and acres of woods isolating the town. There would be no such thing as anonymity, and I didn't know what Briony wanted to do for a living, but regardless, there wasn't much in Peridot Falls for her.

For the most part though, she'd be left alone. As my mate, she wouldn't be challenged unless she wronged someone and Briony didn't seem like the type to want drama.

All I wanted was a quiet life serving my people. I'd had the quiet part down before trouble happened, but I hadn't been much use to the town. My sister had an independent streak a mile wide, and as her twin, Maverick picked up any slack she was willing to give him. That left me with a whole lot of nothing in a small town full of shifters who had their own roles in the clan.

"Why don't you just make yourself comfortable?" Enid

started for the stairs. "I'll talk to Briony, and we'll just wait and see what other trouble DJ is going to start. It's the only thing he's good at."

"He must think he'd be good at leading the pack."

"That boy would do the same to the pack as he does with his females. Run them into the ground until there's no recovering what they once were." She disappeared down the stairs, leaving me alone in a new house with a female stress baking in the kitchen because she didn't want to mate me.

CHAPTER 3

riony

LAST NIGHT, I had finished baking the bars and ate four of them with my sandwich for supper. Levi had kept to his room, and Gran had worked in the backyard. On the outside, not much seemed different. But the handsome shifter inside the house was completely new.

This morning, I dressed in a pair of jean shorts and an old Cougarton 5K T-shirt of Gran's. I wasn't dressed up. I couldn't bring myself to dress differently just because Levi was under the same roof. He'd seen me already. There was no hiding.

I ran my fingers through my hair and inched the door open, listening and sniffing the air for his familiar hint of chocolate-amber scent. Had he even left his room last night?

I thought I'd toss and turn all night, but I slept better

than I had in weeks, as if Levi's presence chased all the bogeymen away. Was he enough to chase DJ away?

I scurried across the hallway and used the bathroom. When I was done, I popped into the kitchen. Maybe I could start the morning whipping up a batch of oatmeal bars? Now that I was up and moving, the anxiety from yesterday curled back into my bones and the need to do something with my hands took over.

My gaze landed on the nearly empty pan of chocolate cherry bars. A self-satisfied smile curled my lips. I knew Gran's grazing habits. She'd cut half a bar here, eat the other half there. She rarely demolished an entire batch of dessert. Only two bars were left tucked into a corner. That had to be Levi's doing.

"Sorry, I meant to stop after the first three rows," he said from behind me.

I jumped, not expecting another shifter to be able to sneak up on me like he had. My pulse spiked, and I gasped. "How did you—this house is as creaky as the old shopping carts at the grocery store. How did you get down here without making a sound?"

I should pat myself on the back. I had been able to finish my entire sentence after my gaze landed on a freshly showered Levi in denim jeans that molded around his powerful thighs. His T-shirt was simply tight, and the abs that rippled through acted like they'd never heard of sugar, much less ingesting over half a batch of chocolate cherry bars.

Humor brightened his already vibrant eyes. "I was already up."

"I didn't smell you." Fire instantly raged in my cheeks. He was probably used to smoother females, more sophisticated.

"I'm not sure if I should take that as a compliment." He

laughed. Then he rocked forward on the balls of his feet. "I smelled you."

I arched my brow, fighting to keep the raging wildfire out of my face. "Compliment?"

He only winked in a way that made my belly flutter before he bypassed me to the other side of the island. "I'm afraid I was a poor guest last night since I couldn't stop eating."

"A baker takes that as a compliment. Besides, you left two."

He grabbed the knife from the pan and wedged the last two bars apart. "You'd better have one or I'll gobble them both up." When he bit into the square, his gaze held mine.

The last thing I wanted to do was eat. I imagined crawling onto the island and laying myself out for him, just like that last chocolate cherry bar.

"I have to get milk." I had to go somewhere else. Being in the same room as him was more disconcerting than it was yesterday.

"I figured. That's why I got ready early."

"Why?" I wasn't usually this slow to process new information, but he was licking the crumbs off the tips of his fingers and I was captivated.

"I'm going with you."

"Do you think that's a good idea?" It was an excellent idea. The mental space that wasn't taken up by Levi this morning had been spent worrying about a simple trip to buy the milk I had forgotten yesterday. DJ had a full night to process what happened in the parking lot. I should've had an idea of what to do, how to move forward, but I was as unprepared as I was yesterday.

Fulfilling a challenge would mean fighting. I didn't want Levi to take on DJ, but I also didn't want to answer for the rage that overtook me when I was shifted and terrified. People would have questions about the past I wanted to stay buried.

I had zero solutions and no milk. I didn't even have another tray of brownies to show for the time I should've been thinking about what to do.

"What do you think will happen if you go by yourself?" He carried the pan to the sink and washed it.

He was considerate too? How was Levi still single? A male who seemed like a dream guy had been driven out of his clan and hadn't found a mate. From everything I had seen, he was a catch. It wasn't like people walked around wondering why I didn't have a mate. They, along with myself, assumed no one wanted me, or that the only ones who did were like DJ and desired to be one step closer to the seat of power. Males who didn't like the idea of an elderly female ruling the pack. Guys who thought she'd let her guard down at a family dinner and they could attack and call it a justified takeover.

The reason why I was still single was even simpler than being guarded. I was nondescript. I wasn't as promiscuous as many females, mostly because I was jaded. I wasn't the fun girl. I liked school, I liked conversation, and even in their twenties, that wasn't what most male shifters were looking for.

I was worried about my heart. I waited until I had left Cougarton to have sex for the first time. I intentionally chose someone who didn't know who I was or what it meant to be Briony Sanders. Then I didn't have to worry about being strung along for who I was. I purposely chose partners who didn't intrigue me. Guys I wouldn't get attached to, so if they ever announced they fucked me because I was Enid Croft's granddaughter, then I wouldn't be hurt.

I forced myself back to Levi's question. What would

happen if I went by myself? "I think DJ is trying to figure out how to get around you. He doesn't want me, so he's going to think of a different way to get to Gran."

"He wants you." He stacked the clean dishes on the drying rack and dried his hands on a nearby towel. He folded his arms across his chest and leaned against the counter, crossing his legs at the ankles.

The whole image was sinful. He'd pulled his hair back into a holder behind his head, revealing the shaved sides. I wanted to run my fingers over the short strands. Were they poky? Would they tickle?

I gave my head a shake. What were we talking about? "He wants to use me."

"He'll do that too, but he wants you. It was in his eyes. His lust was like a cloud hanging over the parking lot."

I snorted out a laugh. "Right."

His gaze narrowed as he studied me. "You don't think you're desirable."

I was standing in front of the hottest guy I'd ever seen. I held my arms out and looked down at myself. He could see what I saw. Denim shorts. Old T-shirt. I knew enough not to wear knee-high socks with my athletic shoes, but I wasn't much more fashionable than that. "I mean... Come on. Who wouldn't want to tap this?" I shimmied my shoulders as if that would make the situation less awkward.

He laughed, but there was a flash of heat in his eyes. He pushed off the counter and prowled closer, towering over me. Gran would be proud I didn't back up. I was more mortified to realize that I wanted to move toward him and not stop until I backed him into the counter once again and scaled his body like a tree.

"You seriously underestimate your appeal, Briony. And that's why you're not going anywhere in town without me."

"Caveman much?" Could he hear how hard my heart was beating? He was so close. His chocolate-laced amber scent closing in around me. His bright eyes pierced me like a stake so I couldn't move.

"I can be." He tilted his head. "But you wouldn't like that. Unless..." He stroked a finger down my cheek. "I bet under the right circumstances, you like being told what to do."

I inhaled a shuddering breath. I caught the word *yes* on my tongue before it slipped out.

Satisfaction oozed into his expression. "I knew it. You haven't had a dominant partner, have you?"

I didn't realize I shook my head until he straightened with a smug smirk. "It could be interesting. You should try it."

"There's been several who wanted to dominate me."

He said exactly what I was thinking. "Ah, but they weren't the right one."

"Well, they've been human."

Shock rocked him backward. "What?"

Before I could explain, the screen door in the back of the house slammed, and I jumped a foot away from him.

"We might have to change that," he murmured before raising his voice. "Enid, good morning. Briony and I were just going to run to the store. Do you need anything?"

Gran rounded the corner and stopped abruptly as if the pheromones we'd been generating formed a tangible wall. "All I need is for you two to be seen together all over town. Hold hands, kiss, hell, make out in the middle of the parking lot. That's what I need for everyone to see."

"Gran!" I said.

With a chuckle, she left the kitchen.

"Well, you heard your grandmother," he said, a grin in his voice. "Ready?"

Levi

Briony insisted on walking to the gas station, which was eight blocks farther away than the grocery store. But I wasn't the one confronted by DJ, so I wasn't going to force her to go back to Teller's the day after. And I got to spend more time with her. The drive would've taken all of two minutes, but her meandering walk would be almost fifteen.

"You grew up here?" I asked as we crossed the street.

"Yes. A farm outside of town."

"It's a lot like home. Fewer hills and smaller trees, but… rural."

She only shrugged, her gaze sweeping around us like she was a CIA agent determining all the places she could run when shit went down. "My dad still lives there, but Gran wanted me to move in with her after I was done with school. I think she was afraid I wouldn't meet anyone out on the farm."

What happened to her mother? If they had killed her to remove another contender for pack leadership, Enid might've killed them. Or Briony's father. But none of the news was important enough to make its way to Peridot Falls. It would be easy enough to look up, and I could also ask Briony, but I didn't want to ruin the lightness we had achieved this morning. Briony was still anxious about any possible run-ins with DJ or someone like him. She may even just be worried about being seen with me. I didn't want to inspect why the thought settled like lead in my stomach.

"No siblings?" I asked.

She shook her head. "Not for me. My uncle and cousin

live on the edge of town and keep to themselves, otherwise Gran just puts them to work around the house."

I chuckled. "I think if humans knew about us, they would be surprised how much alike we are. Whenever I visit Memphis, somehow I end up mowing her lawn or shoveling out her driveway." Which I didn't mind. The tasks barely took a couple hours. The weeks got long.

Her laugh was pleasing to my ears, like a tinkling of jewels from one palm to the other. "I agree. If there's one thing that unites us, it's family drama." She glanced at the houses lining either side of the street, all of them like her gran's. Two-story structures with steeply peaked roofs and tall windows. There wasn't a house on the street less than a hundred years old. "I can't imagine what it's like living in a community with no humans."

"Humans that don't know about our kind," I amended.

"Yeah, I guess that's a major distinction. Most of the humans in town are oblivious of our shifter side. And if they happen to overhear something like DJ's challenge the other day, they just chalk it up to some form of local dialect."

"Do you get along with your uncle and cousin?" I'd only been in town for a day, but I didn't get the impression they had a lot to do with Enid or Briony.

"Uncle Lewis and Gran like to talk politics, but it usually dissolves in bickering. Then Gran tries to needle my cousin Cooper, like she's constantly testing him about his future position in the pack. I told her once that she should just try to be his grandma once in a while."

I stuffed my hands in the pockets of my jeans as we meandered. I didn't know if she was enjoying the conversation or the walk, or if she was purposely taking her time, but I didn't mind.

"My parents were hard on us. We are an isolated clan,

and with Garnet as the closest dragon shifters, I think they worried about our rivalry. Memphis thinks they worried more about intermating."

She focused on me, and I was glad I was intentionally vague. I liked her attention on me. "What difference would that make? Wouldn't it be safer than your clan falling in love with humans and risking them spilling secrets?"

Revealing our secrets to humans was forbidden unless that human was going to be mated to a shifter. It was a catch-22. Did we trust that the human we were committed to felt the same enough to risk our lives telling them about shifters? Because if things went south, it was a death sentence for the shifter who chose poorly. But in this case, that wasn't the problem. "Growing up, there were Brighton Garnet and her sister."

"Oh," Briony said, catching on right away. "Two sons in the Peridot ruling family plus two daughters in the Garnet ruling family equals a combining of two ruling families when your parents probably wanted the population to flourish instead of dwindle."

I could watch her mind work all day. "Brighton's sister was killed when I was a teenager, so it wasn't exactly a worry. And when I'd met Brighton, it wasn't like it was a rampant, undeniable attraction. I think it was the same for my brother. There was no chemistry, and therefore no danger of us moving out of Peridot Falls."

"What are your brother and sister like? I hear about the dragon shifter ruling families, and they're always referred to with awe. What's it like?"

Dragon shifter rulers were the leaders of the shifter world. Other shifters around Peridot Falls were under Memphis's jurisdiction. We weren't royalty, and to humans, Memphis was considered a mayor, but we were their leaders nonetheless. "Memphis and Maverick are a lot alike, which isn't a surprise since they're twins. They're both uptight, can be pricks, and as a kid I made it my goal to crack through their serious shells as often as I could."

"You're a jokester? A prankster?"

The corner of my mouth ticked up. "If the occasion called for it. I got myself in a fair amount of trouble, which is probably why the council came down so hard on me."

Briony's attention was on me, but I couldn't bring myself to look at her. The empathy she emanated soaked into my skin. "They didn't understand you were only doing what you did to cheer your brother and sister up? That's too bad."

"I could've done things differently, but at the end of the day I'm still their little brother, and they still have sticks up their asses." There was that giggle again. I grinned as if I realized the long-honed skill of getting Memphis and Maverick to laugh once in a while was only training for Briony.

"What were some of the things you did to get yourself in trouble?"

There were too many to tell in the few blocks we had left to our destination, but I thought of one story. "One Halloween, I convinced them to go to a club with me in Minneapolis dressed as the three dragons from *Game of Thrones*. And Maverick's girlfriend at the time had blonde hair."

"So she was Khaleesi?" When I nodded, she continued, "I don't see what's wrong with that?"

"Nothing would've been wrong if the costume wasn't really just a giant egg for each of us."

Briony's chortle grew into a full belly laugh until she stopped to lean over and brace her hands on her knees.

Grinning, I finished my story. "We looked more like three Humpty Dumptys parading around Minneapolis.

Maverick's girlfriend was pissed and her grandmother was on the council. They claimed it was a bad look for Peridot Falls."

Briony struggled to catch her breath. "It doesn't scream sophisticated mayor when she's walking around Minneapolis looking like she's ready to scramble." She straightened and sighed, her smile still wide. "That's pretty harmless though."

"I thought so." We resumed our stroll. "I don't think the council really understood what to do with me. Ruling families usually try to have more than one kid, if possible, but I was like the third wheel growing up. The town is already established, so it's not like I can learn a trade and be useful everywhere. Peridot Falls is small enough that if I became, say, an electrician, I would be directly competing against another established electrician."

"And if you offered your services, people might be too wary to turn you down since your last name is Peridot."

"Exactly." I wished the council caught on as quickly as she did. I was in a position going nowhere and taking the blame for doing nothing when they wouldn't allow me to lift a finger.

"Shifters sometimes struggle with change and small towns need to adjust to stay alive."

The gas station came into view around a copse of trees. I was tempted to take her hand, to make this look real, but also because I wanted to touch her. Her cinnamon-sugar smell was so at odds with the smell of blossoms as we walked past blooming flowerbeds, but it worked—like a fancy confection, sweet but with a light floral flavor enhancement.

There wasn't much about Briony I didn't like, it seemed.

"Oh, damn." Briony's gaze was on the parking lot next

to the gas station. A couple of females were talking beside an old but excellently refurbished sports car. I didn't know much about cars, but I appreciated the beauty of the style. "DJ's sister Sasha."

I could pick which one was her. Dirty-blonde hair, arrogant smirk, and flinty eyes. The other female had long black hair, eyeliner as thick as her locks, and an expression that spelled out murder in bold font. "Who's the other female?"

"Her friend Ree. They all hang out together at the garage at the edge of town. That's why I picked this place to grab some milk, hoping we wouldn't run into anyone."

I slid my hand along her back, and she jumped. "We have to make us look believable," I murmured, low enough that shifters farther away couldn't hear my words. She relaxed into my touch, another sensation I could get used to.

Briony tried to make a wide arc around the parking area to the front door, but one of the women spoke first. "I wasn't expecting you to show your face in public so soon." Ree strode past the hood of the car to stand in the middle of the parking lot, uncaring of vehicles pulling in and out around us. She folded her arms across her ample breasts and kicked a hip out. Her gaze slid over me, an appreciative glint in her eye. I didn't reciprocate. "Usually you go into hiding after you're confronted about your weaknesses."

The other woman, Sasha, crossed to stand next to her friend. "Don't you usually wait for your grandmother to fight your battles before you're seen in public again?"

Briony waggled her index finger between the two females. "Do you practice this in the mirror? Do you really try to get it right, practicing different inflections on certain words? Or does it all come naturally?"

I didn't know what I expected out of this moment, but after witnessing how Briony handled yesterday, I should've realized she'd let her mouth fly. And it was glorious. I caught on before the two females that there was no good answer to Briony's question, which she had clearly intended.

Sasha's jaw worked, but she settled on a deadly glare. "You may think you've gotten one over on my brother, but he's smarter than you give him credit for. And I don't give a shit if you're mated or not. I can challenge you no matter what."

"The problem is," Briony said, and I knew whatever came out of her mouth would only dig the hole she was standing in deeper, "that I have better things to do with my time and no one seems to understand that. It is possible to live a life that doesn't revolve around trying to hurt people just to prove you're better than them. Maybe it would be a better use of your time to display other areas you're accomplished in than beating my ass. Because ooh, what a thrill."

How did she do that? Turn the threat around so it looked bad for them? Challenge Briony and Sasha would look like a bully. Shifters prided themselves on their strength and their skill. Beating down an unworthy opponent wasn't inspiring—and would earn them no respect. Challenge Briony and look like a bored female with nothing better to do.

Ree crossed her arms, much like her friend. "You're worthless. You're a worthless addition to this pack, and you're no use to your family." Her lip curled. "What's left of it."

Briony's sharp inhale said the comment hit close to the target, but the hurt radiating from her was a mystery. To me, at least. I was the outsider. But it was clear Ree knew how to hit Briony where it hurt.

"I don't know why you're still in town. You're making everything worse," Ree continued. "DJ was helping you out, you know. At least it seemed like someone wanted you." Her shrewd gaze swept over to me, then returned to Briony. "But I see you have this guy. He doesn't look desperate, but he clearly is. Maybe it's a favor to get him back into his clan, but the sooner you leave, the better off this pack will be. DJ won't have to pity fuck you as a favor to your grandma and he can find a worthy female. He can propagate this colony with stronger shifters than you'd put out."

Waves of anger mixed with pained frustration rolled off Briony. It didn't matter that a person like Ree would say whatever she could to hurt Briony, it was still painful to hear. I rubbed my thumb against the small of her back to let her know she wasn't alone.

Briony lifted her chin. "Someday, you'll talk about a subject you're not completely ignorant of."

She continued toward the gas station, brave enough to finish our mission of getting milk, but Ree didn't let it drop.

"Ignorance is wandering around Cougarton with your mother's killer still out there and not giving a damn. The same thing could happen to you."

Briony flinched under my touch, and rage billowed from her. The force shocked me. I was prepared for her to scurry inside of the gas station or to pivot on a heel and march all the way back to her gran's house. But she didn't. She spun only enough to face Ree and Sasha.

"It'd also be a shame if whoever tracked me down disappeared just like my mother's attacker." She flipped her hair as she turned back toward the gas station and walked away as if she'd forgotten Sasha and Ree existed. My long legs kept pace with her. I didn't have to jog to catch up, but mentally I was spinning on a hamster wheel.

I didn't say anything as she beelined through the store to grab a blue carton of milk and pay for it. I continued to follow her when she slammed out the door and strolled across the parking lot with her head held high.

People watched us. Sasha and Ree had driven off while we were in the gas station.

I waited until we crossed the street to the sidewalk that would take us back to the house. "What the hell was that about?"

"I'm not sure what you're asking. You saw everything that went on."

Was she deliberately avoiding the subject? We walked another block before I tugged on her elbow to stop her. I lifted the milk from her hand because my mom raised me to be a damn gentleman and we were far enough away from the gas station. My gesture wouldn't make her look weak. "What happened with your mom's attacker?"

Her gaze darted around, but we were as alone as we could be on a sidewalk in the middle of town. "No one learned who jumped my mom and killed her." When she paused, I didn't press. Her mother's death still seemed hard for her to talk about. After losing mine, I understood completely. "Ree's aunt used to mess around with my father when he first moved to Cougarton. But then he met Mom and fell in love with her, and they moved to the farm because Ree's aunt was causing too much trouble. And apparently, as she got older and didn't find anyone else to settle down with, she got bitter."

"And you think it was her?" When she nodded, I pressed. "They never found her?"

Her expression shuttered. "We felt it was best to leave

it. Ree's aunt, her parents, and DJ and Sasha's parents—it's like they made their own pack. If they thought Mom had killed Ree's aunt before she died, then it would've been war. We'd lost enough."

There was something she wasn't telling me, but I didn't push it. "I'm sorry."

"Ree's a lot like her aunt. I think that's why there's a lot of hostility toward me other than my seeming meekness. They want my family out of power and they think I'm the weak link."

I narrowed my gaze. Seeming meekness? There was more to Briony than she let on. I was more convinced than ever this female was continuously underestimated. She was intriguing in a way I hadn't experienced before, and she talked to me like a real person. When I swooped through the grocery store parking lot and supposedly rescued her, she didn't treat me like I was a rock star and she was my admirer, but she never treated me like I was worthless.

She might not want me around, but she didn't write me off just because I was the unnecessary Peridot.

I put two fingers under her chin and gently tilted her face up as I lowered my head. Her pillowy lips parted a moment before I put my mouth on hers.

The kiss started slow, gentle. But as soon as her sweet flavor hit my tongue, I swept inside her mouth. I had to know her full flavor. I wanted to drown in it. A little squeak left her and she fisted a hand in my shirt. Tentatively, her tongue tangled with mine, a shy slide, and I was lost. Letting out a growl, I stepped closer, clamping my arm around her waist and cinching her to me.

She gasped and pushed me away. Startled, I almost didn't release her, but my brain came online quickly, sparing me from any danger of pushing her too far.

"Why did you do that?" She was breathless, her cheeks rosy.

What other parts of her flushed when she was aroused?

Because she was turned on. I could smell it. Fuck. Lust coursed through me like I could take her right here, lay her down in the plush green grass next to us and sink myself into the sweet heaven her body offered.

She'd asked me a question, and I struggled to focus. "Because I like you, Briony."

She snapped her mouth shut and hugged her arms around herself. Had I said the wrong thing?

"And you intrigue me. I like talking to you. I like looking at you. And I sure as hell like your desserts."

She shrank in on herself with each point I made. What was I doing wrong?

"Briony," I prodded. She wasn't looking at me.

She finally lifted her brown gaze to mine. "I don't know what you want me to say, Levi. I don't form attachments with guys. I don't trust them. So I'm not sure what the point of all this is."

"What do you mean?"

"This." She fluttered her hands around and wrapped them back around herself. "You have to live in the shifter community, and a shifter community is the last place I want to be."

Right. And we were back to that. I couldn't force her to be with me.

Technically, I could, but I would never. However, there were people in our lives who could order her to be with me, and that was the last outcome I wanted. Forever shouldn't be mandatory.

"I understand." And I really did. I'd grown up knowing I'd never leave Peridot Falls. My evenings and weekends clubbing in Minneapolis were a nice distraction, but I'd also had time to think. And I realized it was pointless. My fate was to live in a dragon shifter community. I couldn't help that any more than I could help how I'd been born. Briony had more freedom than me, and I wouldn't be the one to take it away.

Didn't mean I could bring myself to leave Cougarton. After that kiss, she'd have to order me to go away before I'd leave her. "Look, you could use my help. Let me stay at least until the DJ thing blows over. Then I can go back home." After the parking lot incident, DJ didn't seem like the only threat in town to Briony, but we needed to take one problem at a time.

"Then you can't kiss me again."

"Why? We're both adults and shifters like to have fun." I was curious about her answer. Not many shifters were guarded when it came to sexual activity, but I didn't get the impression Briony messed around.

"The fun part is fine; the shifter part is not. When I can truly trust a partner, then maybe I'll have fun. Until then, it's best to keep my hands to myself."

I groaned as an immediate image bombarded my brain. A naked Briony spread out over her bed, her legs wide and her hand between her thighs. I didn't even know what her bedroom looked like. I hadn't seen her dressed in less than what she was wearing now. But the picture in my head was immediate and crystal clear.

She gave me a suspicious look. "You okay?"

No. Christ, not after that vision. "Yes. How about we see what your gran is up to?"

CHAPTER 4

riony

My lips continued to tingle hours after the kiss in the middle of the sidewalk. Levi was why I stayed away from males I could get attached to. He was the exact reason my heart remained locked in the cage of my ribs. I could fall so easily for a guy like him. He was sweet, considerate, and he made me laugh.

He made me question what I wanted for my future.

I sat at the island in the kitchen with my laptop open, scrolling through schools. After the run-in with Ree, I'd been thinking. Perhaps it was better that I leave town sooner than later. DJ and his family didn't mess with Uncle Lewis. My uncle had rigged his farm with traps. He wanted a peaceful life, like me, but that didn't mean he made it easy to be challenged. I was the easy target, and I was accessible. I should leave.

Pushing my fingers along the mouse pad, I scanned the

list of names of schools. The problem wasn't deciding which city had the master's program I wanted to go to. It was figuring out what I actually wanted to go to school for.

I'd kept my undergraduate degree deliberately general. A business degree had all the basics and was flexible enough to get me into most programs. But at the same time, the thought of taking more business classes made my brain numb. I enjoyed school, but I wanted to do something.

I had to decide what I wanted to be when I grew up. For a girl who couldn't wait to get lost in the big city, I had relatively little idea about what I'd actually do when I got there.

Clicking through descriptions, I let out a sigh.

Levi's voice carried in from the backyard. He'd been outside chatting with Gran while she tended the tomatoes in her greenhouse and dug through her garden for cucumbers. I'd miss Gran and her garden. I'd miss her greenhouse and the fresh produce and herbs she produced for several months until winter descended on the region. There'd be farmers' markets wherever I ended up, but the emptiness inside of me wasn't filled by the idea of other people's produce.

I should learn how to garden. Was there a graduate program for that?

I grew up helping Dad farm, but growing wasn't what I wanted to do, and if I was in a city, space would be limited. Tapping my fingers on the counter, I stared at the laptop screen until it blinked out. Crap. I tapped the mouse pad to wake the monitor up. The back door opened, and Levi strode in. The expression on his face was almost contrite.

Before I could ask what was wrong, Gran breezed past him, a cucumber in each hand. "Before you get upset with him, it was my idea."

Closing my laptop, I swallowed the rising tide of anger. Gran was meddling. Was Levi in on it?

Grimacing like he didn't want to be the one to deliver the bad news, he said, "I got a call from Lachlan Jade, and, uh, he said my brother was coming to Jade Hills for a visit. I figured I should go down there and see them both."

Since he'd been sent to Jade Hills to be somewhat of Lachlan's protégé. Made sense. He must've gotten friendly with the Jades. "Okay?"

"I think you should go with him." The nice thing about Gran was that she didn't beat around the bush. Direct and fast, like ripping off a bandage.

"Why would I go with him?" I asked.

Levi scratched the back of his neck. The sunlight streaming through the kitchen danced over the glossy black of his hair. It was hard to tear my gaze away to look at Gran.

"There's trouble brewing here." Gran was serious now. "Levi told me about the gas station." She gave me a pointed look as if chiding me for not informing her as soon as I entered the house. I should've but I'd trained myself to stay away from thoughts about Ree and her aunt. "It's not going to die down while you're staying with me, and he's under the same roof. I don't trust DJ or his sister, and I definitely don't trust Ree. Too much like their parents."

But to go to Jade Hills? Why didn't I just stay with Dad for a while? What would I do with the Peridot brothers and Lachlan Jade? Bake them cookies to eat during their meetings? "What would my role be?"

"You'd be seen around with Levi. Shifters will start to think of you as off-limits."

I snorted a laugh. "So, what? I'm going to be his arm candy?" I snickered again. I wasn't arm candy material.

Gran's gaze flickered toward him like she couldn't read him. Neither could I. Why would he want me along?

"I'll let you two talk about it, but think of it as an order from me." She deposited the cucumbers by the sink and left the kitchen, presumably to call Lachlan directly and inform him I would be traveling with Levi. I could act as her liaison, but I doubted she had business with him.

Levi slid onto the stool next to me. His chocolaty amber scent curled around me, and I'd be happy to marinate in it all afternoon.

I tried to wrap my head around the problem I had identified and wasn't prepared to handle. I was becoming a burden to Gran, and I needed to leave town. Levi would drag me along on business. Granted, business was a strong word. He was visiting his brother. Like me, there wasn't much for him to do. I guess we both had that in common.

"I don't know..." I didn't know. I didn't know what to say, what I'd do, or how I could be useful. Familiar frustration crept up my spine. I hated feeling helpless. When I felt helpless and lashed out, bad things happened.

"I don't either. We'll figure it out, don't worry. But I think leaving Cougarton for a while is a good idea."

I rested my elbow on the island and propped my head in my hand. "How long has it been since you've seen your brother?"

"A few months, I suppose. We're not particularly close."

His wooden tone drove my curiosity. "Wasn't it just the three of you?"

"Maybe it would've been different, but since he and Memphis are twins, it was always like they had their own language I couldn't translate."

The third wheel when the other two were a perfect set. That would be hard. I'd been lonely growing up as a shifter in a mixed human-shifter town. Dad worked the land every day, and by the time I was old enough to drive, I was the girl who'd missed school for a week after finding her mom dying in the ditch. I was related to the pack leader, but I was anything but a role model. People didn't know what to do with me. Story of my life.

"I'm sure the trip will be fine." My gaze strayed to where Gran had left the kitchen. "She's probably right. It's best if I leave town for a while."

The confrontation earlier this morning had shaken me. I had been so close to saying something stupid I couldn't take back.

"Lachlan and Indy are good people. You'll like them. They're as drama-free as you can get. Well, after Lachlan killed her ex-boyfriend and she killed that guy's mother. Everything is pretty quiet now."

Laughter bubbled out of me. That sounded the opposite of calm. I had overheard Gran and my uncle talk about the goings-on of dragon shifter communities. She'd talked about the deaths in Jade Hills, and from what I understood, they were both justified.

"Sounds more mellow than it'll be here if I stay." I gave him a sunny smile that I hoped would cover my simmering anxiety. My goal had always been not to create more conflict. I didn't like fleeing, but I also didn't want to drag my issues around behind me. I'd like to be excited I was going on a road trip with a handsome male who kissed like a wet dream, but I needed my baggage to stay behind. And I needed to keep from falling for Levi more than I had.

~

Levi

. . .

HAVING Briony in the seat next to me for an hour and a half was a special kind of torture. Her cinnamon-sugar smell filled the cabin of my car and the shorts she wore rode up every time she shifted in her seat, baring more inches of that creamy skin I wanted to lick.

Her kiss was sweet as the brownies she'd made. Would the rest of her taste the same?

The magnitude of how much I wanted to know staggered me. And if I kept thinking about her bare flesh, my lust would soak into the leather of my seats and become permanent.

"What would you have done if you hadn't had to return to Cougarton after college?" Jade Hills was still a half hour away, and we'd only chatted about superficial things. She'd asked me about Peridot Falls, and I'd asked her what it was like growing up in Cougarton. Her dad still farmed, but she talked like she wanted the opposite life. Big city and concrete.

"I would've gone right into a master's program."

I wasn't surprised. She seemed like she'd rather be buried in books than deal with people, yet I couldn't put my finger on what her actual interest was. A lot of the girls I met when I'd been clubbing in Minneapolis were her age. They were entering careers or finishing up degrees at various levels. One thing I'd learned was that when they were passionate about something enough to continue going to school for it, they liked to talk about the subject. Future doctors would turn from flirty to analytical in a heartbeat. Future CEOs bragged about knowing a second language—learned specifically for business and they'd say "bottom-line" and "let's circle back." And then there was the one girl who had bought ten different drinks, lined them up in front of her, and proceeded to taste each one, smacking her tongue and lips in between to determine what exactly was in the mixture and if she'd change any of the proportions. Then she'd circle back to the top flavors. She probably owned a distillery or a franchise of bars by now.

But with Briony, I couldn't tell. "What do you want your master's in?"

"Well..." She flashed a sheepish grin and averted her gaze to stare out the passenger window. "I'm interested in everything, so that makes it a hard decision."

"You don't know what you want to be?"

Briony was the most even-keeled female I'd come across. The women at the clubs, they'd been out for the night, looking for a good time and to maybe hook up. I had been glad to be there for both. It was like I lived vicariously through their drive and optimism. The youngest of three with no role in his clan. But where Briony had the seriousness the other women ditched at the door of the club, she was missing the focus. An unusual combination.

"I mean—I want to be..." She slumped in her seat. "God, I don't know. All I knew when I went to college was that I wanted to get away. A bigger town, surrounded by people who don't know me. I guess that's the same with the master's degree. It's the best way to justify leaving my dad and gran."

Her raw confession hung in the air between us. She was as aimless as me. I had expected to go to Cougarton and meet a spoiled female who'd gotten whatever she wanted, a girl who shunned her role in the pack and refused to play by shifter rules.

And that was what I'd found—sort of. I'd found a female who didn't care for the violent part of shifters, and a whole community who wanted to exploit her peaceful nature.

She didn't shun shifters' baser drives out of some

superiority complex. No, she'd seen the toll it took on a family when a young girl lost her mother. She knew what it was like living under the stress of constant violence. Gran could be in a fight while we drove on a gorgeous summer day to another town to visit my brother. The stress of losing her family wore on her, as did the distance it created between her and her uncle and cousin and her gran.

And that was why she didn't want to be with me. "But you're determined that wherever you go is a big city?"

Nothing personal. But the band tightening around my chest didn't know the difference.

"It's one of the advantages of not being a dragon shifter," she said. "You can't promise that no one will bother us in Peridot Falls. And I can't promise that I won't say something blunt, and then someone will have something to prove, and I'm right back where we started."

"I understand." My hometown was a quiet community. We didn't like trouble, so much so that other clans thought of us as arrogant. We kept to ourselves, much like Briony. And people thought we must assume we were better than them.

Logically, I understood everything she was saying, and I supported her. Emotionally, I was a caveman who wanted to drape her over my shoulder and carry her off where no one could bother us.

I'd been salty as hell toward Memphis for bringing up the idea of mating a cat shifter. Now, she owed me for meeting the girl of my dreams I couldn't have.

The rest of the trip went by quickly. I drove through downtown and parked at the coffee shop on the edge of town. The armory turned city hall was about six blocks away, but I'd grown fond of caramel macchiatos while I'd been here.

Briony peered out the window. "Why are we stopping here?"

"It's almost lunchtime, and Lachlan likes to meet with Indy over the break. I don't think either of us wants to walk in on that."

"That's sweet."

"Yeah, it is." I wanted a marriage like Lachlan and Indy's. Not the miscommunication and hurt that they'd gone through the first years they were together, but what they had now was magical. Lachlan was content to stay in Jade Hills, work in his office, and spend time with his mate. Soon, they'd start having kids, and he'd thrive with all the extra joy that brought.

Lachlan had been a mentor to me before I'd gotten to know about his personal life. He'd taken me under his figurative wing in Garnet River, helping me and my sister out when Peridot Falls council wished to make me an example. And then in Jade Hills, he hadn't acted like I was a pain in the ass. He also hadn't treated me like I knew nothing about being a member of a ruling family.

He had sent me to the surrounding shifter communities, especially the dragon shifter clans, to introduce myself and get to know the other clans. My visits weren't just to kill time. Peridot clan had been isolated for several years. Dragon shifter clans tended to concentrate in rural areas, but the isolation of those towns was rapidly disappearing. Yet in northern North Dakota and over the border into Canada, there wasn't much industry beyond agriculture, and the billionaires hadn't gobbled up the land yet.

While Garnet River and Peridot Falls were alone together in north-central Minnesota, the shifter communities in the neighboring state were thriving. They were able to go into business easier together and to intermate, something my community had been missing out on for decades.

Briony and I got out of the car and walked into the coffee shop. Lacey, behind the counter, grinned and pointed at me with both index fingers. "Caramel Macchiato is back in town."

"I couldn't stay away. No one else makes them like you."

Briony lifted a brow toward me but her attention was stolen by the goodies display. She crossed to the plastic case and peered inside. "You make all of these in-house?"

Lacey sidled over to stand directly in front of her. "I give myself one macaron weekend a month to try different flavors, otherwise I cook small batches of the most popular flavors. But I might be expanding if I can figure out the mail order side of macarons."

"I'll take a box with one of each flavor." Briony straightened. "Mail order? Is there a lot of demand?"

Lacey nodded, her eyes bright and her smile wide, as if she was thrilled to find someone who wanted to talk about the business side of baking. "Oh, yes. Gift boxes, holidays, what have you—every baker puts their signature on their chosen dessert, so as long as you can find a way to get your goodies in someone's mouth, you might be able to convert them to a regular customer. I want to try free sampler boxes, but I've got to figure out how not to go in the hole first."

"Like running a sale and including the sampler as a free add-on?" Briony asked.

"Exactly." Lacey grabbed a pink box and folded it into a neat rectangle, then started to select one of each flavor of macaron to put inside. "Online, I'll tie my product to a sale, but I might travel around to fairs and trade shows and set up a booth." She set the box on the counter. "Want something to drink?"

Briony glanced at me. "I guess I need to see what macchiato is all about."

Lacey laughed and bustled behind the counter getting our drinks ready. I shoved my hands in my pockets and watched, amused, as Briony perused the entire shop. She inspected the shelves piled with candles and homemade seasoning mixes, then moved to the bookcase filled with canned goods, each with Pride of Dakota labels plastered on them. As she walked to the other side of the coffee shop, she trailed her fingertips over one of the refurbished wooden tables Lacey's mate had made especially for the building.

She stopped, facing a wall full of pictures with little sayings. Each picture had a tiny price tag hanging off the corner. She chuckled at one that read, "All I need are the three *C*'s: cats, coffee, and chocolate."

She chuckled, then caught me watching her.

"Charming, isn't it?" I asked.

"Yes." She crossed to stand by me. "I like how everything adds to the ambience, but it's also for sale."

"Businesses have to be just as crafty in small towns. They might not have as much competition as a big city, but they also have a smaller customer base."

"I was thinking the same thing. I never put much thought into the businesses at home, but now I'd be interested in roaming downtown with a new perspective." There was disappointment in her tone, like it was a nice thought but not feasible.

"Except you can't really roam in Cougarton and be left alone."

She rolled her eyes and nodded. "Yep."

Her need for anonymity stemmed from the way she was messed with because of her grandmother. If she was in a town where it didn't matter, would the population size make a difference?

My hopes were slowly rising until I recalled her comment about suspecting attitudes would be the same if she was the mate of a ruling family. And she wouldn't just be my mate, she would be my *cat* shifter mate. Many dragon shifters had a superiority complex, and they'd be dicks on a good day. But there would be those who resented the idea of what they perceive as an inferior shifter mating into a ruling family. They'd want her to prove herself, just like the residents of Cougarton.

My mood turned sour just as Lacey appeared at the counter with our cups. "Are you in town for a while?"

"A day or two. This is Briony Sanders from Cougarton."

Briony stiffened. Not enough that Lacey could see it, but I could feel her reaction to being outed.

Lacey hit her forehead with the palm of her hand. "I should've introduced myself. I'm sorry—I'm used to everyone being all up in my business."

"Please, I didn't think to introduce myself either because of the same." The tension in Briony ebbed, and I liked having her so relaxed next to me.

Lacey grinned and snapped up a business card to hand to Briony. "I'll have my samples process figured out soon. Check in and I'll be happy to send you some."

Briony clutched the business card like it was a precious gift she feared would get stolen away. "I'll have to wait until I'm out of Cougarton or the cost of international shipping would be too much."

Lacey leaned over the counter with a conspiratorial wink. "I have connections with guys who regularly travel over the border. It'll be no problem."

Briony was still smiling as we walked out of the coffee shop, the card still in her hand. "She was nice."

The lilt in her voice finally made the details click together in my brain. She probably hadn't had many friends growing up, and she certainly didn't have any in Cougarton as an adult. Maybe she'd met people in college, but being a shifter would've meant there was a natural separation between the friendship bond.

"Not every small shifter community is going to be hostile toward you," I said after we got into my car.

Her gaze snapped up to mine, and she narrowed her eyes like she knew what I was getting at. "But I'm also not mating one of the Jade brothers."

"They both are mated."

"If common sense was that abundant, I wouldn't have had issues in Cougarton."

I couldn't argue with her observation. All I could do was remind myself that she couldn't be mine.

CHAPTER 5

riony

THE SHORT CAR ride from the coffee shop to city hall was quiet. Something I said had disappointed Levi, and he'd shut down after I pointed out that no dragon shifter community would be safe for me if I was mating one of the ruling family. Was he disappointed? I couldn't believe he would actually be dejected about me not mating him. Perhaps it was his pride? A guy like him shouldn't get rejected by a girl like me? I hadn't gotten that vibe from him, but I also didn't know him that well.

My traitorous brain pointed out I knew him better than any guy I'd ever dated. The trip to Jade Hills hadn't taken long, but we'd talked about everything and nothing. Our conversation had been light, not delving into significant topics.

But we'd had those talks already too. Like when he'd driven me home from Teller's after DJ's challenge. And later in my kitchen. Yesterday, when he learned his brother was visiting Jade Hills.

I was confused. Levi was turning into everything I wanted while being the opposite of what I had planned for my future. Would seeing him with his brother help confirm that we weren't meant to be?

I set Lacey's business card in the console and eyed the big building in front of me. Jade Hills City Hall had been an old armory. Levi said Lachlan and his brother Ronan had converted the place into a decent city hall and the second level was a furnished apartment for guests.

A few cars and a pickup were also parked in the lot. Levi parked next to the truck. "Ready to go meet everyone?"

My anxiety kept my butt planted in the seat. "Who's everyone?" I had met Lachlan once but he'd been in cat-shifter territory. He'd seemed okay. On the serious side, but he also hadn't enforced a mating order between me and Levi. He had the pull with the Silver clan leader who ruled all of us.

I didn't know Maverick. What would he think of me as a choice? Not good enough for his brother? Not good enough for a Peridot? I shouldn't be worried anyway. We'd already established it wouldn't work out.

"I don't know," he answered. "Probably Lachlan and Maverick. Maybe Indy."

Three dragon shifters didn't sound so bad. I could tell from the way Levi talked that he had a ton of respect for Lachlan. The tinge of disappointment in his voice when he spoke about Maverick wasn't aimed toward his brother. I got the impression he wished they were closer. Levi thought he was the third wheel.

I felt like the same today. I was only temporarily shoved out of my town by Gran, but it gave me a sense of what

Levi must be going through. He'd been away from home for a couple of months. He didn't seem eager to go back, only because he wanted to return and make a real contribution. Until then, he appeared to be searching for himself. And wasn't I in the same position?

I blanked out all my insecurities as we entered the building. The area was so quiet, only the sounds of birds and the wind rustling the leaves of the trees surrounding the property greeted us.

Inside, I was hit with the smells of different people. Pine-covered-hearth scent that must be one of the males. A lighter fresh smell. Was Indy Jade here as well? And a vanilla-amber scent. A pleasing odor, but not one I wanted to roll in and bare my belly at like Levi's.

If I had been in my cat form on the ride here, I would've purred the entire way.

I couldn't meet Levi's brother and the ruler of Jade clan with my cheeks flaming red. I pushed those thoughts out of my head and lifted my chin. I was Enid Croft's granddaughter. These people did not want to fight me, so the least I could do was be a decent guest.

Levi led me through the armory with its white-tiled floor and plain walls to an office. Lachlan sat behind a simple wooden desk. He was a handsome male with sandy-blond hair, trimmed short, and eyes the color of the gemstone his clan was named after. I hadn't met Indy before, but I assumed it was her reclining against the window ledge with her leg propped up. Her expression brightened when we walked in.

Maverick's resemblance to Levi was uncanny. Or would that be the other way around since Levi was younger? Maverick's hair was as dark as Levi's but shorter and without the undercut. He kept the length longer than Lachlan's and the short cut made the angles of his face more severe but in a good way. His eyes were as bright yellow green as his brother's. The brothers were close to the same height, but Maverick had a stockier build, more like Lachlan's.

"Levi!" Indy pushed off the ledge and swept around the desk to give Levi a quick hug. "I wasn't sure you were going to come back before you went back to Peridot Falls." She turned toward me and stuck her hand out. "And you must be Briony. I'm Indy Jade."

I wasn't used to being eye level with shifter females, much less taller. Indy was only a couple inches shorter than me, but the relaxation sweeping through my body had more to do with her ready smile and her genuine enthusiasm at seeing us.

"Nice to meet you," I said. "Thanks for letting me tag along."

"Oh, anytime. It's so nice to finally get visitors and not be the clan everyone's sick of." She went back around the desk and stood next to Lachlan with her hand on his shoulder. His movement was hardly noticeable, but he leaned into her touch.

I wanted that. Lachlan and Indy were clearly in love. His expression was permanently hard—except when he looked at his mate. Could I find a guy who looked at me like that?

I wanted to think so. Maybe the real question was whether or not I would find someone like that in the city. And if I did, he would most likely be human. Telling a man any kids you had would turn into a mountain lion was a big obstacle. Right after convincing him I also turned into a mountain lion. It didn't matter I preferred sunbeams to killing bunnies, it's a hard concept for humans to handle.

I could skip all that and agree to be with Levi. Was he

only open to the idea because I was against it? If I said, "just kidding, I changed my mind," what would he do?

No, there was still the problem of Peridot Falls and how they'd accept me.

Maverick rose like a dragon unfurling his wings. I didn't mean to creep closer to Levi, but I took a step before I stopped myself.

Maverick's smirk was good natured. "It's not easy being the only mountain lion shifter in a roomful of dragons, huh?"

"They prefer cat shifter," Levi said after he clapped his brother on the back and nodded a greeting at Lachlan.

Maverick frowned and somehow it made him better looking. The vanilla-amber scent belonged to him. Even combined with his looks, I still didn't want to rub myself over any furniture that smelled like him. But as soon as I got back in Levi's car, I'd have the urge to do just that.

"Is there a difference?" he asked. "Doesn't it make it sound like they're a house cat cleaning their ass in front of the picture window?"

"That's just your cat, Maverick," Levi joked. "They're efficient people. Fewer syllables."

I add, "Otherwise we get into arguments about whether we're pumas, cougars, or mountain lion shifters. Cat is a nice catchall."

Maverick's snort wasn't derogatory. "Cat shifters do kind of like to fight about everything."

"Agreed," I said.

Lachlan waved to the empty chairs. As we were sitting, he said, "Maverick isn't just here for a vacation. He wants to evaluate how other shifter communities are sustaining themselves."

Humans were strongly discouraged from moving to dragon shifter communities. Simply, they weren't allowed unless they were mates. I would be happy to tell him about Cougarton and even the small community I grew up in, but he'd need to find options that would either bring dragon shifters to the community or businesses that could be run by those who were already there.

I listened, fascinated, as Levi chatted about what he'd seen during his visits to Silver Lake, Gemstone, and Penopal. Lachlan and Indy chimed in with what they'd seen come and go in the community. Most of the mentions had closed down, thanks to the way Lachlan's parents had ruled, but new ones like the coffee shop were doing well.

Indy glowed as she described her latest project. "We've almost got one cabin complete. Penn has the online infrastructure built so we can rent to only shifters. We'd be happy to share the setup with the other clans."

Lachlan dipped his head. "Absolutely. It would be Jade's way of paying back the harm they caused in the past."

"Peridot Falls could support cabin rentals." Maverick spoke without including Levi. "Without the cost involved for IT, we just have to plan for construction, making sure we don't impede on residences and our own private recreation areas."

"I think the money would be best utilized building up the downtown first," Levi said. "Otherwise, where are all the renters going to get their food? They're on vacation. They want to grill or eat out, and all we have is Macey J's Corner Store and Honor's place. We're close enough to Garnet River that we could lose the business to them."

Maverick waved his hand, blowing off Levi's valid points. "Then we'll place the rentals as far away from Garnet River as possible."

"Then we're pouring money into roads. The other side of Garnet River is woods."

Maverick's expression grew annoyed. "Do you want Peridot Falls to succeed or not?"

"Of course I want it to succeed." Levi's tone was laced with long-held patience. He was used to his siblings dismissing him. "But I don't think rushing to do what Jade Hills is doing is the answer. We need to look at what our community's specific needs are."

Maverick ticked off his fingers. "We need money filtering into the town. We need more people moving in. We need more businesses."

"We need to make sure the town can support those businesses moving in," Levi countered, "and the downtown would be a better place to start."

I wanted to reach over and squeeze Levi's hand. I agreed with him. I had heard Gran discuss pack politics and the community. Dragon shifter rulers functioned as their clans' mayors in the eyes of humans, but they still performed the work of a mayor. Gran was on the city board, and when she'd talked about her frustrations or the support for the decisions made, I'd been an avid listener, curious about how issues were discussed and solved outside of fighting.

Maverick needed to listen to his brother.

But he continued to shrug off Levi's attempts to redirect his focus. "We'll see what Memphis says."

I didn't have the patience of Levi. "Will she listen to you over Levi? Is that why you're waiting to see what she says?"

It was like the air got sucked out of the room. My only lifeline was the delighted lift in Indy's brows and the gleam of approval filtering through Lachlan's gaze.

"What do you mean?" Maverick spoke evenly, but I heard what his words didn't say. He knew damn well what I had meant, but he wanted me to be blunt.

If that were the case, I'd like him more. I hadn't met

many people who preferred blunt Briony. "From what I know, Levi has been traveling around communities with the intent of bringing back useful advice for his own. He's speaking from a place of experience, and after growing up in a household associated with pack leadership, I happen to agree with him. If I were to talk to my gran, I think she'd have the same advice. But..." This was where being blunt got tricky. "I think you're used to dismissing Levi because he's your little brother. You're not used to adult Levi who wants to contribute as a member of the ruling family. So what I mean is that you need to get over yourself."

Maverick's expression grew impossibly harder. Levi sat unmoving. Had I upset him? Or worse, embarrassed him? That wasn't my goal, but I wasn't the type of person to sit around being frustrated when I was in the position to speak my mind.

So much for being a decent guest.

"I need to get over myself," Maverick echoed. He rubbed his bottom lip between his thumb and forefinger, his forehead furrowed. "I have an ex-girlfriend who told me the same thing." He slapped his hands on his thighs and looked around the room. "This girl doesn't know my brother like I do, but I am aware that I don't know him like she does. Perhaps a brainstorming session before we return to Peridot Falls is in order."

The tension drained out of the room, and I could finally take a full breath again. I chanced a peek at Levi and found him watching me, appreciation buried deep in his chartreuse irises.

"Levi, what do you say?" Lachlan asked. "Can you and Briony stay for a couple of days, maybe take Maverick to visit the other clans and talk commerce with them?"

So far, being in Jade Hills has been a better experience

than living with Gran. I wasn't in a hurry to get home. When Levi arched a questioning brow, I nodded.

Indy clapped her hands together. "I'm still giving you both a tour of the cabin rental sites whether you want it or not."

I chuckled, looking forward to my time here. The traitorous thought crept into my brain. What if I was just as welcomed at Peridot Falls? What if I found being there a lot better than my hometown and Cougarton?

And again I reminded myself I wasn't mating one of the ruling family in Jade Hills. I couldn't risk it and I refused to live looking over my shoulder like I had growing up. And there was no way I would stick around the dragon shifters to find out who Levi ended up with. I didn't need that heartbreak.

~

Levi

MAVERICK and I came up with a quick game plan while still in Lachlan's office. We had decided to spend the rest of the day in Jade Hills, touring future camping sites. Tomorrow, we'd head to Silver Lake, and the day after we'd go to Gemstone. From there, Maverick could head home, and Briony and I would go back to Cougarton.

My brother was reclined in his chair, long legs sticking out and crossed at the ankles. "Why would you head back to Cougarton? If Briony is going through all the data with us, wouldn't it be beneficial to have her come to Peridot Falls? We could even stop in Garnet River for a quick look at their progress."

A resounding *yes* echoed in my head. I wanted to keep

Briony with me. If her cinnamon-sugar scent faded in my car, my brain would equate the loss of her smell with losing her. So logically, if I kept her with me that meant she was mine.

"I don't want to be a bother," she said, her hands folded tightly in her lap. I couldn't tell if she was screaming *no* inside her head, or if she really wanted to see this brainstorming and research-gathering phase through. Both?

"You are helping us out. You're one of the most objective opinions we can get." Everything I was saying was true, but I really didn't want her to go back to living with Enid. I didn't want her to be back within reach of DJ and his sister and her friend.

"Agreed." Maverick sat up, slapping his boots on the floor. "So… What are our arrangements while staying here?"

"There is the apartment upstairs," Indy said, pointing toward the ceiling. "And there's our house. We have two extra guest rooms."

"The apartment is a one-bedroom," Lachlan added.

Before I could figure out a way to stay in the one-bedroom apartment with Briony because I was a selfish prick, Maverick spoke. "It makes sense for me to stay here. Levi and Briony can take the bedrooms in your house."

Damn.

Indy grinned, excitement dancing across her features. "Our first guests in our new house." She squeezed Lachlan's shoulder like it was a big deal, and when thinking back to how they'd been before they reconciled, it probably was a momentous occasion in their lives.

"We can go ahead and get the tour out of the way." Lachlan rose, immediately putting his arm around Indy with his hand coming to a rest on her hip. I itched to do the same with Briony. To have my hand rest on her tantalizing curves.

We filed out of the office. Maverick hopped in Lachlan's pickup with Indy, and I got back in my car with Briony. We hadn't been out of the vehicle long and our scents were still mingled together. I inhaled deeply. The rightness of the blend settled inside me and I had to quash a low, approving rumble.

Did she sense how well we went together too? Was it more than stubbornness? Was her insistence on moving to a big city nothing but an old ideal she clung to because the other option was scarier?

No matter what, it wasn't for me to decide.

I followed Lachlan's pickup out of town. "I appreciate your support back there."

She let out a nervous laugh. "I thought I overstepped. I wasn't sure how your brother was going to react."

"Honestly, neither was I. I'm used to standing up for myself but not hearing anyone else do it."

She peered at me, but I kept my eyes on the road. "Really?" she asked. "Everyone just assumes you don't have anything beneficial to say?"

I shrugged without taking my hands off the wheel. "For a long time, I didn't."

"Or maybe you got used to being talked over, and you quit trying to add to the conversation."

Her words touched home. I had tried to be helpful with our parents, but it had been in the form of chores. I mowed the lawn, chopped wood, hunted, and learned how to do minor work on our vehicles. My dad wouldn't let me do too much. *It's good to be self-sufficient, son, but there're mechanics in this town trying to feed their family. We'll take it to the shop.*

By the time Maverick and Memphis moved home from

college, it was my turn to go. And then Mom had died—hit by lightning during a freak thunderstorm—and Dad had made sure he followed soon after.

When I returned home after college, Maverick was too busy helping Memphis keep the clan on the right track. They hadn't had time to train me. Anything I could add, they had already thought about ten times over. So, yeah, I eventually quit trying to be helpful and made myself scarce in an attempt not to be a burden.

"I'll have to remedy that," I said. "But I need to be more informed now than I was back then."

She pulled out her phone and started tapping through the browser. "Maybe we could start by making a list of different businesses in the surrounding communities."

I peeked at her screen. She was pulling up a map to learn what towns were nearby.

"I've heard so much about Silver Lake. I'm kind of excited to go."

The Silver brothers were decent guys—the opposite of a male like DJ. Deacon Silver and his human wife, Ava, would make a good dragon shifter impression on Briony. His younger brother Steel still lived and worked in Silver Lake with his wife Avril and their new baby girl. The youngest Silver brother lived in Jade Hills. Lachlan thought he'd stop over at the house tonight.

"You'll like Deacon and Steel Silver. Their youngest brother Penn lives in Jade Hills, and we should visit with both him and Venus. She's owned her own salon for years, and Penn runs all of his online education courses out of his house. Many of the clans are using his services."

Briony's fingers flew over the screen of her phone as she took notes. "I'm going to make a file for each town, and then we'll add each business and jot down notes as we go." She rolled her gaze toward me and smirked. "But it'll just be between us. In case we have anything critical to say."

I laughed, liking how easy it was to be with her. "Absolutely. I know how you hate to be abrasive."

She let out a theatrical gasp. "Levi Peridot, how well you know me." She focused back on organizing her notes tabs, but her grin stayed in place.

The Briony I had met had been serious. Her light-brown eyes had been full of worry—for herself and for her gran. The Briony outside of her pack was fiercely loyal, but there was a lightness about her that I hadn't seen often enough in Cougarton. Gran had been right. Briony had needed to get away from town but not so tensions could die down. Briony needed to get outside of the city limits in order to be herself. She needed to laugh again without worrying it'd be seen as weakness. She needed to be able to confront males in powerful positions without the typical backlash she'd been facing. Maverick had been a good target. He was used to Memphis's strong personality and hadn't been phased by Briony's insistence on including me.

Lachlan turned off the road, and I had to focus on the rough gravel path that carved through the trees. I wished I knew whether I would be thanking Lachlan or cursing him for encouraging me to meet Briony. Because the longer I was around her, the more I was certain she was mine. But that feeling meant nothing if she refused to be with me.

Briony

I HAD SPENT the day riding around with Levi. Lachlan and India showed us and Maverick around Jade Hills. I'd been enjoying myself then, and when Indy invited Venus and Penn to their house for dinner, I'd had the best time I could remember. Laughter and teasing between Venus and Lachlan reminded me of my mom and uncle when I was a kid. Uncle Lewis and Cooper would come over and visit. Cooper and I would play, then we'd have a family meal just like this. Uncle Lewis would joke around with Dad. Mom's laughter rang in my head.

I missed her. The night she was taken from us changed everything about my life.

We were on the back deck of the house with all the lights off. All of us could see just fine and the bugs stayed away more in the dark. Crickets and frogs buzzed in the background and stars dotted the sky.

Venus was practically sitting on top of her mate. "Briony, did they get a chance to show you all the trails we use when we shift?"

I nodded. I rarely shifted into my cat. My hometown was rural, but a mountain lion sighting could cause chaos. Besides, it wasn't safe to run in my animal form when a farmer or rancher could see me. They didn't take threats to their animals lightly, and mountain lions were definitely a threat to calves, herding dogs, chicken flocks, and anything else we could hunt that would taste yummy in our beast form. "It's been forever since I've shifted."

Her brows lifted. "Then you definitely have to. We don't isolate ourselves in the middle of nowhere surrounded by trees for nothing. You've gotta enjoy the perks while you have them." She patted her hand on Penn's thigh and his muscles twitched under her touch. "Speaking of which, want to go for a hike before we go home?"

The hungry expression on his face announced they would be doing a lot more than hiking. Venus's lips curved into a slight smile and she grabbed his hand.

"Hate to eat and run," Penn said as he followed Venus off the deck and through the yard to the trees, "but I'm forever at her mercy."

Venus waved at us over her shoulder. "Bye."

Lachlan tossed them a small wave and grunted. "He begged to be at her mercy. Steel said it was a glorious thing to see."

Maverick rose and stretched his hands above his head. "I heard so much about her—I never would've guessed she would end up with the youngest Silver."

The story of Venus's love life had rippled through the shifter community. Her mating to Deacon Silver had been arranged since she was a kid, and then he'd mated a human just before his thirty-fifth birthday. Dragon shifters, especially the rulers, were forced to mate before they were thirty-five. They had higher levels of aggression than the rest of the shifter population, and their wild side could be tempered with a mating.

Maverick and Levi were single. Levi had almost seven years before he needed to worry about the deadline, but Maverick had to be approaching the deadline. Yet I didn't sense instability from him. I definitely didn't get the impression he was a guy who easily lost his temper. But perhaps that was why the rest of the dragon shifter population got to skate past their deadline birthday for a few years before it was harshly enforced with termination. Ruling families were often made the example. Something I could empathize with.

"They're perfect together," Indy said about Venus and Penn. "But Penn will make sure he's perfect for her no matter what."

Maverick's lips twisted. "Good for him, but I'm never going to be that guy. Relationships are supposed to be about compromise."

Levi chuckled. "Yeah, but the female's not supposed to be the only one making concessions." Maverick shot him a scowl, then shrugged. There was definitely a story there I would love to ask Levi about. Would he tell me?

Would we be around each other long enough for me to hear about what was going on with Maverick?

I smothered my frown. I didn't like the idea that my time with Levi was limited.

Maverick jumped off the deck. "I'm going to head back to town. My car's still at city hall, but I need to run after all that driving."

Indy smiled and pushed off Lachlan's lap. "I'm heading to bed, but don't take it as a sign of curfew. Come and go as you please."

"I might take a quick run." Levi stood, towering over me. The thrill traveling through my belly couldn't be denied. My cat liked a big male over me.

My cat was keen about Levi in a way she hadn't been about any male I'd been around.

Indy said her good nights and Lachlan trailed after her inside, holding her hand.

"You heading into the woods?" Levi asked as he stepped out of his shoes.

"I'll sit out here for a bit." Lachlan looked like he was about to gobble Indy up. I'd hear less outside.

Levi jerked his shirt over his head. A jolt made me sit up.

"What are you doing?" We weren't in public, and we were shifters, but he wasn't stripping down, was he?

The thrill from earlier roared back, ringing in my ears. My pulse hammered and if I was in my cat form, I'd be panting.

His grin flashed in the moonlight. "Going for a hike. Can't tear my clothing while I shift, can I?"

"N-no," I stuttered. He was really undressing. Right in front of me. I was sitting down, at even level with his— "You can't just undress on the patio." I couldn't keep my voice calm. I sounded as panicked as I felt.

His grin only widened. "I'm a dragon shifter. Don't cat shifters just undress when they're ready to shift?"

"I don't know. I never went running with my pack."

His smile dimmed, like I had missed out on something special. "Then come running with me now." He unzipped his pants, a wicked gleam in his eye. But he turned around, presenting me with his tight ass. "I won't look while you undress."

"You can't turn into your dragon on the patio. The stonework…" I was reaching for excuses and I knew it.

His chuckle reverberated into the night. "I don't plan to. But you can change into your kitty on the stones." And then he shoved his pants down and I was presented with hard glutes. A dimple curved through each cheek and my hands lifted before I slammed them onto my lap. What did I think I was doing? I couldn't touch his bare ass.

He stepped out of his pants and shoes while I was riveted to the bronze skin and carved muscles in each leg flexing and bunching as he moved. The dark hair scattered over his legs made me think his chest had a smattering of hair on it too and I damn near purred in appreciation.

Making a disgusted sound, mostly to pretend like I had some control in the situation, I stood and fisted the hem of my shirt.

As I was about to whip it over my head, Levi jogged off the patio and into the middle of the yard. He tipped his head back like he was stargazing. Was he going to shift? I had never seen a dragon shifter change forms. I hadn't seen many of my own kind shift either. Not since my mom died, and I turned my back on everyone like me.

The way his smile had dropped when I admitted I didn't run with my pack gave me enough courage to take my shirt off and step out of the rest of my clothing. I wasn't bold enough to walk closer to him as a naked female, so I let the change take over.

As my bones contorted and shifted, creating a painful yet pleasurable stretch, like I was finally using muscles I had ignored for too long, I wondered what the process was like for a bigger shifter. Was it more intense for bear shifters and dragon shifters to turn into a creature so much larger than their human selves?

Oddly enough, I would feel comfortable asking Levi these questions, but I was a mountain lion now. Trotting off the patio and across the grass, I was pleasantly assaulted by the same smells that had been present all night but were more vibrant, more alive, more colorful. Including the naked male in front of me.

His chocolate-laced amber scent rolled over me, and I paused as if I was going to flop myself onto my back and bare my belly like a house cat.

Get it together, Briony. I was going on a hike with a dragon shifter. Yes, it was unusual in my life. And yes, I was growing more excited by the second. But I couldn't lose my composure.

Would it be an issue if I did? Nothing about my personality turned Levi away. If anything, he grew more determined to learn about me, about why I behaved the way I did, and why I had made the decisions I had. The feeling that I could talk to him about all this stayed with me as I sat on my haunches next to him.

"I'll shift closer to the trees," he said and started walking toward the opening of a trail wide enough for a dragon, thanks to Indy and Lachlan.

I hung back and watched, fascinated, as his skin

darkened and changed into green scales and his body grew into a sleek dragon with webbed, talon-tipped wings. His long neck was slender and graceful, but his eyes, while larger than when he was in his human form, were Levi. He blinked and shook his head, creating a ripple down his back, as if he had to mentally adjust to being his creature.

I shook myself and stretched until my front legs were straight, as if I had to get used to my form as well. In truth, this felt good. It had been a long time since I ran my cat, and even longer since I had been shifted without worrying about being challenged or attacked. I was an easy target and I knew it.

But it was different in Jade Hills, and it was different around Levi.

He swung his head around and blinked at me as if to ask whether I was ready.

I dipped my head and rose to all fours while letting my tail hang like a curved check mark toward the ground.

I expected him to lumber, but he moved with ease along the trail, minimizing sound by stepping lightly. He kept his wings tucked close to his body, and I wished I could watch him fly. A lot of shifters took our ability to change forms for granted, but I didn't. I loved the speed and agility of my cat, and I enjoyed the freedom of living in both worlds while also hiding our secret from humans. I couldn't imagine being able to fly on top of that.

Unable to suppress the sense of playfulness that surged inside of me, I darted around Levi, threading through the trees until I popped out onto the trail in front of him. A low growl made me start and spin around, but I only saw humor in Levi's gaze. The peridot-colored sheen gleaming over his scales was both subdued in the dark of the night and more apparent in the shadow of the trees. He was a magnificent creature.

When I turned to look down the trail, I gave in to the energy flowing through my skin and bones and bounded down the path. Leaves whispered against Levi's scales, letting me know he was following me.

I didn't know how long we ran for, and I didn't care. The air was fresh, and the trees gave us all the concealment we needed. Following along the loop, I decided to run for a few more minutes before turning around to go back. We had a full morning planned. But after a hundred yards, the trees thinned out. I slowed to a stop, and Levi did the same behind me.

Dark, twinkling water spread out in front of us. A lake. I recalled Indy mentioning there were a few small watering holes and sloughs scattered through the woods when we were at the lake near the cabins she was building.

I glanced back at Levi and he fluttered his wings as much as the trees would allow. A dragon's version of a shrug?

Just as I was about to decide to turn back—better safe than sorry—a dark form swooped out of the sky and skimmed above the surface of the water. His scales were just as dark as Levi's, and he had the same peridot sheen over his body. Maverick.

When Maverick pulled up from the water, he didn't rise higher than the trees, but instead swooped to the side, staying low to the ground, until he landed right in front of us. His sides were heaving in the excitement and his bright eyes were undeniable. He jerked his head toward the water like he was inviting Levi out to play.

The wall of heat behind me vibrated with excitement. I stepped to the side, making room for him to dart into the open and fly with Maverick. A wave of excitement swept through me. What would the two of them do?

Levi launched himself into the air. Maverick took off

after him. I prowled along the shore with my eyes to the sky. The enhanced night vision of my cat could make out each dragon. They were similar in size, but I could tell them apart. A human would have to be close to the area in order to make out their forms.

The guys stayed close to the tops of the trees, flying down until their talons dragged on the water's surface before angling up again. They were fast, their wings stretched out. The webbing helped them blend into the night sky.

I approached the edge of the water and crouched to sniff the surface, my nose filling with the fresh smell of the lake algae and detecting the other animals that had been by recently—rabbits, turtles, and the sharp musk of a porcupine.

When I lifted my head, Maverick zoomed in front of me with Levi almost literally on his tail. White teeth gleamed as Levi playfully snapped at the barbed end. A growl rumbled through the night, but I didn't detect animosity. The sound of a dragon's laughter?

Their speed slowed and Levi circled above me, dropping lower until he landed at the edge of the shore. Maverick looped up, giving us a nod and disappearing over the tops of the trees.

Energy sizzled over my body, relaxing my hackles that would have otherwise risen. When I glanced over, Levi was in his human form. And naked.

I swung my head back around, wishing my eyesight wasn't that good, but even in my human form, in the dark, his image was branded into my brain. Strong, wide shoulders. A lean, muscular body, tapering into the legs I had admired earlier. Only this time, he was facing me, and when I looked, I'd gotten an eyeful. His impressive package was just hanging there, at my eye level, and he acted oblivious to it. Something that was impossible for me to do.

The night was cooler than daytime had been, but a wave of heat rolled over my body and my fur coat felt ten tons heavier than normal. I padded into the water.

"That was fun." The sounds of water splashing resonated behind me. Was he following me in?

He continued past me, not stopping until the water was up to his waist. Then he turned to face me, an amused tilt to his lips. "Go ahead and shift back. Unless your cat likes to swim."

I had frolicked in ponds when I was younger. I liked to play in the water as much as the next cat shifter, which wasn't a lot. But as a human, I enjoyed swimming—in a swimsuit. Usually, any other swimmers were also wearing some sort of covering. And if they hadn't, I likely wouldn't have cared.

I cared about Levi's nudity way too much.

His smile broadened and he pushed back until he was floating on his back but mercifully keeping his hips below the surface. "Come on, Briony. The water's deep enough out here to cover your tits—although I won't complain if you want to show them off." He tipped his head forward, a naughty gleam in his eyes. "I'd like to know if they're as spectacular as I think they are."

He'd been wondering about my breasts?

I took a couple more steps, the water sloshing under my belly. Any farther and I would either need to swim as my cat or shift. The way Maverick and Levi played in the sky streamed through my brain. They'd been having fun. I wanted that same lightness, and I'd have a better time if I shifted into my human form.

Making the decision before I could talk myself out of it, I closed my eyes and let the change take over. Too late, I realized I would only be in knee-deep water once I was in my human form. Midshift I tried walking farther into the lake. But I was unprepared for the difference between a cat's footing in water and my human feet on slippery rocks. Combined with my near panic at being naked in front of a floating Levi, I tripped and fell face-first into the water.

Scrambling against the slimy rocks of the lake bottom and the weeds tickling along my arms and legs, I kicked to the surface. Strong hands gripped my waist to help keep my head above water as I sputtered for air.

"Shit, Briony. Are you okay?"

My feet could touch the bottom, but that likely meant a significant part of my body would be in the open air. I bent my knees and bumped into Levi. He was standing close, and when I blinked water out of my eyes and regulated my breath, I was gazing right at him.

"Yes?" I gasped.

His soft chuckle was still full of concern. "Are you sure? I don't want you to get hurt."

His hands were still on me, and when I pushed my drenched hair out of my face, he seemed reluctant to let me go. But he didn't float farther away. He stayed crouched in front of me with his knees on either side of mine.

"I've never shifted in the water. I wasn't prepared."

His eyes twinkled, more yellow under the moonlight. "It doesn't help that you're shy."

Despite the cool water, a blush heated my body. "I'm not shy. I'm... insecure." The admission was raw. I had never thought of myself as insecure. I thought I looked just fine. Was I stereotypically beautiful like many other females? No, but that didn't bother me. I refused to be jealous over nature. I liked my plain brown hair and my complexion that didn't leave me thinking I needed bronzer, concealer, or powder. I liked being me. The part of my life that made me insecure was other people. I was aware they didn't think as much of me as the rest of the females in my pack, or in other packs, but that didn't mean I wanted to hear it. None of it meant I wanted to face ridicule for something as simple as being myself.

"What do you have to be insecure about?" His brows dropped down and droplets of water sparkled along his face. The dark hair I thought of running my hands through way too often was pushed off his face.

"Other people."

"Fuck them."

I laughed and pushed away to flow through the water before I did something impulsive like throw my arms around him. "That's the same thing I said to myself, but you saw how that turned out."

He swam after me, only his head bobbing above the water as we made our way toward the middle of the lake. Algae quit licking at my ankles and the temperature of the deeper area dropped a few degrees. This was a small lake but a deep one.

"I didn't see much as you were falling." He swam closer and his voice dropped. "But I saw enough. You have nothing to be ashamed about."

My cheeks were burning. After falling in, I probably looked like a half-drowned rat. "Uh, thanks."

He tilted his head and inspected my face. "You don't know how to take compliments, do you?"

I shrugged as I treaded water. "I'm not used to them, I guess. Not about my looks."

He drifted closer. "I noticed you when I first drove into Cougarton."

All I needed to do was change the angle of my treading

hands and I could put distance between us, but I didn't want to.

"This sexy little thing crossed the street, right in front of me, and I had to follow her into that parking lot." From the way his searing gaze was boring into me, I knew he was talking about me but the information was having a hard time registering. "Your hair glowed like spun gold. And your eyes glittered like gemstones. Do you know what that does to my dragon?"

He wasn't talking in the past tense, but I still couldn't buy into what he was saying. "Actually, there's a jewel tone for all our hair and skin colors. From obsidian to topaz to—"

"I'm talking about *your* hair and *your* skin color, Briony. I want to tuck you under my wing and make you mine."

A tremor went through me, getting lost in the waves rippling gently around us. I wanted to be his. I wanted it to be easy, just like it is now, in the dark, by ourselves. "I want..."

He closed the distance between us, water swirling over my breasts and shoulders as his warm hands clamped around my waist, jolting me with a heat-filled buzz. "What do you want?" he asked softly.

"I don't know," I said as I wrapped my arms around his neck. My breasts smashed against his hard chest. He paused as if stunned I made such a bold move, but he recovered quickly and pressed his lips onto mine.

The kiss in the middle of the sidewalk had nothing on this. The combination of cool water and hot bodies swirled together until a desire-filled cyclone raged around us.

When he opened his mouth, I greedily accepted his tongue inside, lapping against it like I could never get enough. He slid a hand down my body, instantly heating me where he touched. If this entire lake became a hot tub, it'd be because of him.

I didn't know how we stayed afloat, but we did. I clung to him like he was my life preserver and we were in the middle of the ocean. I wrapped my legs around his waist just as he cupped his hand between my thighs and stroked his fingers through my seam. A shudder racked my body, and he broke the kiss enough to say, "I've got you."

"I know," I whispered and rode his hand as much as I could, bobbing with the gentle waves.

His hips moved under my legs from the rhythmic kicking he was doing to keep our heads above water. I would've gladly sunk to the bottom if it meant his finger could keep strumming my clit.

"Levi," I gasped, my lips brushing against his. My breath was coming quicker the closer he stroked me to a swift peak.

"I've got you," he repeated like he knew I was in danger of losing myself and floating farther away.

I was connected to him, but at the same time, I felt rudderless. Lost. I knew exactly what I wanted, and at the moment, it seemed to also cost everything I wanted. Nothing made sense but at the same time it was all perfectly understandable. And as long as I was hugging Levi and his rigid erection was wedged between us next to his arm while he stroked me off, I was fine. But once I exploded, I would have to try to understand what all this meant. I would have to admit that a guy didn't bring a girl to meet his friends and his brother and go on late-night walks with her for nothing. I'd have to admit that Levi might genuinely like me, and that I could possibly be walking away from someone who would be good for me and good to me.

Someone I could easily fall in love with and forget all the plans I had made.

I cried out against his lips, a combination of passion, frustration, and desperation. "Levi?" I didn't know what I was asking him, or what I was trying to tell him by repeating his name, but the arm he had wrapped around me cinched me to him.

"Let yourself go, Briony. Let me see you fly apart."

He had me, and that was both the problem and the solution.

The climax crashed into me with the force of a tsunami, the total opposite of the small waves rippling across the surface of the lake.

My moans were swallowed up by the night. I didn't know if anyone was around to hear, and I didn't care. On any other night, with anyone else, I'd be mortified—but I also wouldn't have come this hard. The male holding me was responsible.

When I came back to myself, my grip on Levi loosened while I clambered to come to my senses. The moonlight cast harsh shadows across his face, making my belly flip with his intensity.

I brushed a hand up his cheek and pushed back a wet lock of hair that had fallen on his forehead. "Wow," I murmured. Aftershocks vibrated through my body.

"That was so beautiful I think I need to do it to you again." The intensity of his expression and the determination in his tone told me he wasn't joking.

I didn't know how we weren't sinking like tombstones tied together. He was rigid from head to toe and the erection pressed between us pulsed with the suppressed force of an imminent volcanic eruption. "You're serious."

He changed the angle of his kicking legs and propelled

us toward shore faster than I thought possible. "If I'm not inside you within two minutes, I'm going to go feral."

Delicious tremors licked through my body. We hadn't planned what we had just done, but the logistics of the rest were failing me. "Here?"

"Nobody's around, and if they are, fuck 'em. I want to be buried deep inside of you, feeling your body milk mine the next time my name leaves your lips."

This male wasn't the laid-back Levi I'd gotten to know. This male knew exactly what he wanted, when he wanted it, and it was me.

"Where are we—"

His feet hit the bottom, and he swept me up and out of the water. I yelped, tightening my hold around his neck. He strode to shore with strong, confident steps. I would've slipped and fallen at least three times by now. Several feet from the water's edge, he dropped to a sitting position, keeping me on top of him.

"Aren't the rocks cutting into you?" My knees hit the larger pebbles of the beach, but I wasn't concerned about myself.

"I can't notice a damn thing with you spread over me." He gripped my hips and lifted me until the broad tip of his cock pressed against my entrance.

I went rigid, my hands gripping his shoulders, and stared at him, wide eyed. Was it possible I'd only met him a couple of days ago and now he was almost inside me. Should I wait? Would I survive a delay? "Are we really doing this?"

"We can hike back to the house. Just say the word." He was as rigid as he'd been in the water. His ass was on the ground and his knees were raised in the air. I could sit on his thighs and take a moment, but anything other than sinking onto him and taking him completely inside of me wasn't an option.

But I couldn't just ram myself down onto him. He was bigger than all the other guys I'd been with, and I was likely more inexperienced than many of the females he'd been with. He'd make sure this was good for me, but I wanted to… I didn't know. Did I want the sex to be so spectacular he'd never get over me? Did I want the fireworks between us to convince me that living a life in Peridot Falls and watching my back was worth it? Did I want a fuck so good I didn't have to think about a thing?

Yes to all of it. I swirled my hips, coating his tip with as much of my wetness as I could before I sank onto him an inch at a time.

"*Fuck*, Briony. You're wet and tight and this is just…" His fingertips dug into my hips, and he watched the point where we were connected. His abs were clenched and his pecs were bunched. "That's it. Take it all."

I let a long sigh escape into the night and settled on him, loving how full he made me, reveling in the connection, the heat, the energy racing between the two of us. I barely noticed the shivers creeping over my skin from the cool night air hitting the wet droplets covering my body. I was surprised the two of us weren't steaming.

He brushed his hands up my torso and palmed each of my breasts. "Now ride me."

~

Levi

SHE BARKED out a cry and her body clenched around me tighter than a vise. She was hesitant at first. I worried the rocks were digging into her knees, that I should end things and whisk her away to a more comfortable spot, even if moving risked killing the mood. But then she started rocking those sweet hips of hers, gliding up and down my length in a way that wiped all other thoughts from my mind.

"That's it," I murmured.

Her body was hot and silky and I couldn't quit fondling her tits. They were perfect handfuls, spilling over my cupped hands in a way that made my mouth water. I released them in order to watch them sway and bounce in front of my face.

"Take everything you need," I said as I rubbed my hands over her hips and ass. Christ, I loved her curves.

"I think I'm going to come again," she panted.

"Yeah, you are," I groaned, barely able to retain a shred of control. Blistering heat flooded between us and she was clenching me so tightly I could barely see straight. When I looked at her face through my haze of lust, I caught her uncertainty. Clarity returned. The sex wasn't all about me, and she looked almost worried. "Have you ever been with a shifter?"

She rose up and slammed back down, eliciting a moan from both of us. "No. It's never been this strong before."

And it was likely she'd never come twice before.

I gripped her hips again, taking over the pace so she only had to think about her pleasure. "Let it go. Just let yourself enjoy it."

She rolled her head back, her wet hair falling off her shoulders, and steadied herself by propping her hands behind her on my knees. "Levi, god, I'm going to come again."

And if there was a next time, I would show her that orgasming three times was also possible. "Let it go. You're so fucking beautiful, I want to watch you, again."

It must've been the right thing to say. She arched her back, shoving her tits into my face, so close I nipped lightly at a nipple.

She barked out my name, her body going rigid, and I buried my face between her glorious breasts and let myself hit my peak. I hollered into her fevered skin as I came. She'd have my handprints on her ass, and I liked that idea a lot.

When she finally came down, letting her weight rest on me, we caught our breaths together. Until she went rigid with a gasp. "Oh my god." She scrambled off my lap, scraping her creamy skin on the small rocks.

"Be careful," I warned, worried for her while wondering what was wrong.

She looked down at her lush, naked body, then her gaze swept across me. I rose to my feet, my flagging erection preparing to stand tall and proud since she was still so close.

"We didn't use protection."

Shit. I was better than that. I was always more prepared. "Are you on anything?" Shifters didn't have to worry about STDs with our natural healing abilities.

She pushed her hair off her face with a trembling hand. "I think… I think I forgot to take my pill the last couple of days with all the shit going on."

If it wasn't for her reaction, I wouldn't be bothered. In fact, it was dangerous for me to think of her carrying my child. I was ready to be mated, to start a family of my own. Granted, I wanted to wait until after I had more of my life together, but that was me. Briony had plans. And none of them included me or Peridot Falls.

"I'm sorry. Really, I wasn't thinking, and I should have done better."

My genuine concern seemed to calm her. "I should've

thought of it too. It isn't only on you." She hugged her arms around herself. "I'm not in heat, so the chances are slim, but still..."

The only reason I was grateful for the worry over our lack of protection was that she wasn't self-conscious about her nudity. It still broke me that she was closing in on herself. Cat shifters went into heat and pregnancy was more likely, but I hadn't been concerned about the details since I hadn't known many cat shifters, much less dated them. "It's okay. Next time, we'll use protection."

A light flush spread across her collarbones and crept up toward her face. "If I were to get pregnant, it would be a dragon shifter baby. I'd be stuck in Peridot Falls." Her voice wavered. "I can't believe the possibility didn't even occur to me."

I wanted Briony—craved her—but I didn't want her as my prisoner. Dragon shifter young could only be raised in a dragon shifter community. Kids were too unpredictable. If the mother wasn't a dragon shifter, she'd have to move. Shit could get messy for her while I'd be continuing on like normal. "I'm sorry."

"I can't believe I didn't even consider using something." Her eyes misted over and she blinked back tears. "I need to go."

I opened my mouth to keep reassuring her it was okay, that we'd learned our lesson and we wouldn't be overtaken by mindless lust again, but before I could, she shifted into her cat. Her soft skin turned into fur and her limbs morphed into that of a big cat's. She took off running.

Stung that she was so terrified of being isolated in Peridot Falls with me that she panicked and ran after the best sex of my life, I stared at the moon shining on the surface of the lake. It wasn't my life at the mercy of change; it was hers.

Stepping forward, I was going to shift and go after her, make sure she was okay, but I stopped. She needed space from me. I started the walk back to Lachlan and Indy's place. The pebbles turned to dirt and after a few yards, I was crunching through the undergrowth of the woods, sticking to the trail we had followed to get here.

By the time I entered the clearing around the house, she had dressed and gone inside. I grabbed my clothes and was covered by the time I reached the back door.

Inside, the place was quiet. I went to the guest room at the far end of the hallway. Lachlan and Indy were either already asleep or remaining quiet to keep from bothering us. The cinnamon-sugar smell stopped at the first guest room door. I was tempted to knock and ask if she was okay, but my intuition told me I had done enough.

She wasn't in heat, but if she had been—we'd have been more out of control than we had been. The what-ifs scared her. I scared her.

I closed the door to my room and stood with my back to the cool plank of wood. When we'd been connected, I had thought we had a shot. Maybe things could work between us. The level of chemistry we had was undeniable. It was once in a lifetime. But I'd been wrong.

CHAPTER 6

riony

I FELT LIKE A FOOL, and I had acted like an eighteenth-century virgin. But I hadn't been able to escape the fear piercing my body when I realized we'd forgotten protection. Cat shifters went into heat, and while my body lit up like I wanted to shove my ass toward Levi when he was close, I wasn't in fevered heat. But he'd taken my concern seriously and instead of brushing me off, he had attempted to understand the situation. Handling my feelings would be so much easier if he wasn't such a good guy.

Levi wasn't a snake in dragon scales. He had swooped in to help me. The fact that he had driven to Cougarton to meet me in the first place said a lot about his character. He had likely heard I wasn't worth the effort. Dragon shifter communities might not be as familiar with me, but shifter communities knew me. My name was likely accompanied by an eye roll.

I stared at myself in the guest room mirror. Hair of spun gold. Said the male with hair of polished onyx. The description sounded like I'd walked out of a fairy tale, but I was just a normal girl. A boring woman who could turn into a big cat.

My mind wandered back to the day my mom was killed. I hadn't been a normal girl that day. Levi scared me, but I'd terrified myself that day. I'd understood how I could ruin my family.

I slid my lower lip through my teeth. I had grown up not wanting to be alone. I had wanted the love I'd witnessed between my parents. And when Mom died, I had changed, and I told myself my dreams had changed. The more I had endured from my own pack for withdrawing the less I had wanted to do with males and shifters altogether.

But I didn't feel that way around Levi. I enjoyed being with him. Talking to him. And what we had done in the water and on the beach… it wasn't so hard to believe his feelings were genuine when I quit listening to all the insults flung my way over the years. I was a strong female, a strong shifter even, and it wasn't my problem what people thought about me. However, it became my problem when I let it affect my happiness.

I had to do something about that.

My stomach was a knot of nerves when I swept out of the bedroom. Movement and voices were coming from the kitchen.

"Maverick said he'd meet us at city hall." Levi's voice rumbled over my skin, transporting me back to last night. The hardness of his body against mine, the open way he focused on me, unashamed about his attraction. "If, uh,

Briony doesn't want to go, I can visit the local businesses with him before we go to Silver Lake."

"Why wouldn't she want to go?" Indy asked.

I swept into the kitchen before Levi had to make excuses. I couldn't blame him for thinking I'd hide out in my room all day or make up reasons to avoid him. "I'm going. No rest for the weary."

Levi's bright gaze jerked toward mine. His surprise wasn't about me bursting into the kitchen. After fleeing, I pranced into the kitchen like I didn't have a care in the world. I gave him a smile, trying to communicate my regret without words while also showing him I was genuinely happy to see him.

I'd never get tired of looking at him. He hadn't pulled his hair back yet. Silky black strands hung over his forehead and right eye, shadowing the chartreuse and adding a mysterious edge.

"Perfect," Indy said as she dished out scrambled eggs onto four separate plates. The smell of bacon clogged the air. Lachlan was hunched over the pan at the stove.

My stomach rumbled, and I pressed a hand to my belly, adopting a sheepish grin to hide my nerves. Before I ate, I had to talk to Levi. I couldn't run from him like he would shatter my world and then pretend the sunny day was glorious and I couldn't get enough of him.

"Do you mind if I steal Levi really quick?" I asked, letting my smile die. "I need to continue a conversation with him that we started last night."

Indy's gaze jumped between us but she didn't appear surprised. They had been quiet in their bedroom when I had returned after being at the lake, so they'd either noted we had returned separately and assumed there was a reason why, or the tension between us today was thick enough to stab a fork into. "Absolutely not. You two can head out to the patio. You'll get a little more privacy that way."

Lachlan arched a brow over his shoulder and returned to moving the sizzling bacon around in the pan.

Grateful they weren't making a big deal about the thick atmosphere between us, I followed Levi out to the patio.

He turned, wrapping a hand around the back of his neck. His shoulders hung like the weight of all dragon-shifter kind was on him. "I really need to apologize again—"

I flung my arms around his neck and slammed my lips against his. It wasn't quite how I wanted to start this talk but going to sleep alone in my bed after the most powerful sexual experience of my life made this move more urgent.

He snaked an arm around my waist like he was afraid I'd slip off and hurt myself but his body remained stiff.

I broke the kiss. "That was a poor apology for how I reacted last night."

His brows knit together. "What do you need to apologize for?"

"For not believing you."

"About what?" He shook his head but didn't release me. "I don't mean to be a dunce, but—"

"You're not. I lay awake, terrified I made a mistake and then I wondered… What if I didn't? What if you really see me and I've been surrounded by so much bullshit I can't tell what's good for me and what's not?" I pushed the hair off his face, loving how the soft strands ran through my fingers. "Don't get me wrong, I'm not ready to be a mom yet, but I let the shock be an excuse to ditch you, and that was wrong."

"What are you saying?" His eyes were searching mine.

"That I want to give us a chance." My bravado failed me

and I loosened my hold on him. "That is, if that's what you want."

He tilted forward and lifted my chin with his index and forefinger. His hair fell back over his face as he leaned down to place a gentle kiss on my lips. This was it. My freak-out last night scared him off. Or was the sex spectacular in my mind but mediocre in his?

Oh, shit. I didn't think this through.

"I want you, so yes," he said as he straightened, taking my hands in his. His gaze swept the lawn, then darted back to the sliding door. "And if we were alone, I'd show you how much."

A grin spread over my face and euphoria could've lifted me off the ground until I floated away. "Okay." I didn't know what else to say, but I desperately wanted him to show me how badly he wanted me.

A smile crinkled the corners of his eyes. "We should stop for condoms today, but I can't think about more beyond that." His eyes smoldered. "I can't risk getting hard right now. So…which shifter community should we buy them in? We can't disappoint your gran after all. Maximum rumors need to get started."

Usually, I'd hate the idea of people talking about my sex life. But when it came to Levi, suddenly I didn't mind. "Let's buy a pack in every town we stop in."

He laughed and draped an arm around my shoulder. "I like the way you think."

I melted into his hard body as we walked into the house. I didn't know what our future held. All the same issues were there, but I knew I couldn't give up on Levi and that was a start.

Levi

While I wanted to ravage Briony now that she had given us a chance, the day after our interlude on the beach left us little time to ourselves. Maverick left his pickup parked at city hall and hopped in with me and Briony. Today, my brother was the third wheel. Only, unlike me, he was oblivious to it.

"Maybe this place will have some decent coffee." His mood had gotten crappier as the day went on.

I was starting to expect the excuse he had given for visiting Jade Hills was bullshit. Something was going on with him, and he wasn't talking. And since I doubted he would tell me around Briony, I played along. "Silver Lake has a bakery downtown. I'm sure you'll find you something."

He grumbled. When I glanced in the rearview mirror, he was staring out the back window. Briony sent me an amused look from the passenger seat. I wasn't sure she had figured out what Maverick was up to, but she likely sensed something was eating at him.

It wasn't the lack of caffeine. As much as I had wanted to stop at Lacey's, we decided to visit Silver Lake for the day. Briony and I could make a good show of being together, since we were actually together.

I had a girlfriend.

How did that concept turn me into a fifteen-year-old? I had dated McKenzie in high school. The first and only female who could be called a girlfriend until now, and she'd had a thing for Maverick even though he'd been in college. In those days, it'd been nice to have more to do than fuck around with the guys and get into trouble, so I'd ignored my gut feeling. Then Maverick had met Astra and

McKenzie cried an entire weekend. For my pride, I'd had to break up with her. She had been my one and only attempt at a relationship.

I bypassed the exit for Silver Lake, driving on the highway until I reached the turnoff for a long driveway. Deacon had said to go to his house first. Ava was working in the yard all day, but she wanted to meet Briony, and they'd ask Avril and Steel over.

As I pulled up in front of the house, a big male with wavy dark hair and stormy blue eyes walked outside, wearing blue jeans, a loose gray polo, and no shoes. A human woman popped out from behind him. The shade of her hair was similar to Briony's, golden-brown strands glinting under the sun.

I parked behind one of the garage doors, and by the time I got out, Deacon had already introduced himself to Briony and Maverick.

He nodded toward me. "Nice to see you again, Levi. I'm glad you took us up on the offer to come back."

"Have to show my big brother how popular I am," I joked.

The grumpiness from earlier was gone from Maverick's face. He was back to being just another charming Peridot brother. "I wouldn't believe it if I didn't see it. Everyone in Jade Hills knows who he is. I'm starting to wonder if I'm related to a celebrity."

If my brother kept going, I would be in danger of blushing. He almost sounded proud. Didn't he think I knew how to people? He'd never gone to Minneapolis with me. He only knew the me that hung around city hall and tried to help him and Memphis but was only seen as the annoying little sibling even when I was in my twenties.

But Maverick could be turning on the charm for the crowd. He probably didn't mean it.

And as always, I would do my own thing. Except Briony wrapped her hand around the inside of my elbow. She wasn't the most touchy-feely female I had met, but that was her personality, and I wouldn't hold it against her. It also made moments like this more poignant. It was like she could sense what was going through my head and wanted to support me.

"I hope you all came hungry," Deacon said. "I know you want to go explore the downtown businesses, but I wanted to show some Silver hospitality first." He glanced over our heads. "There's Steel and Avril. They're bringing the rest of the food."

I looked forward to hanging out at Deacon and Ava's home longer, but I was growing antsy. I had been in no rush to get home before I met Briony. Being with people who didn't treat me like a nuisance when I was a grown male capable of a whole lot more than they gave me credit for was nice.

But the urge to return home hounded me. I was from a ruling family. I couldn't be gone from my clan long. Not unless I moved because I had mated. And now that Briony was giving us a chance, I wanted to rush through the rest of the steps.

Steel parked next to me and rushed around to help his mate get their daughter out. Once introductions were made and we all lost Maverick while he cooed over the baby, Deacon led us around his house to his back patio. The smell of hickory wood chips filled the air.

"Are you smoking something?" I asked.

He grinned and went to the silver smoker next to the grill. "It's my new toy. Ava bought one for me after we cleaned the bacon supply out of the grocery store when we had a family gathering. Now I have a deal with one of the local farmers and we smoke the meat ourselves."

Briony released me to drift toward Ava and Avril, mostly because Ava had been beckoning her over. They took a seat on the stone bench built into the edge of the patio, and Ava excitedly asked Briony questions about herself and her life.

Confident Briony could hold her own, especially around females who genuinely wanted to get to know her, I turned my attention to the others. Maverick and Steel had joined me and Deacon by the smoker. The way we grouped off and were chatting and laughing reminded me of growing up.

A hard hit of nostalgia punched through my chest. My parents used to invite friends over, and I'd trail behind Memphis and Maverick, wanting to be involved in whatever they and their friends were doing. When my parents died, that had stopped. Memphis wasn't the type to have large gatherings at her home, and sometimes I suspected Maverick was so tired of being a different person around everyone that when he was at home he just wanted to be his normal moody self. And if he wasn't with Astra, then he was brooding about why he and Astra had broken up. Their on-again, off-again relationship made my head spin.

"This'll double as a quick business meeting," Deacon said, and Steel nodded, crossing his big arms over his chest.

Steel's gaze strayed to his mate and daughter, softening when it touched on Avril and damn near melting when it landed on his baby. Resistance was breaking down inside my chest. I hadn't allowed myself to think much about a mate and family. If it happened, it happened, but I had also known the likelihood of finding what I was looking for in a nightclub in the middle of the city was low. Meeting like that was probably fine for humans, but unlikely for shifters. Casually dating didn't compare to introducing someone to a whole new world they could never tell anyone about, and once they learned about shifters, there was no leaving the world.

I had plenty of years before I reached the mating deadline. The last few years I'd been finding my own way, instinctively knowing a guy coasting through life wasn't good mate material. I had wanted to plan and have a role before I tied myself to a female.

Other than the order of my birth, I didn't have that yet. But thanks to Briony's interference, maybe Maverick would step out of his big brother identity long enough to see I could have a legitimate job in the community.

When Lachlan offered to let me stay in Jade Hills while he mentored me, his words weren't an empty promise. I'd worked with him in his office and traveled through the nearby shifter towns, getting to know people, learning how to be diplomatic, and forming an understanding of the individual needs of each community. I was excited to go home and find ways to benefit my own town. I just needed Memphis and Maverick's support.

Steel opened the smoker and a chorus of groans rang out as the delicious smell of meat hit our noses. Deacon chuckled while he worked knobs on the smoker and hauled the ham onto a platter. We were a rapt audience, and out of the corner of my eye I caught Briony's gaze searching for the source of the savory smells. We shared an amused look, like *meat and shifters, am I right?* When I turned my attention back to the group, I caught Maverick staring at me.

He dropped his gaze, the corners of his jaw clenching, and focused on Deacon. "I thought since I was here we could talk about the new education systems being implemented thanks to Penn and how we can use it to create more jobs in the community."

Deacon let the ham rest while he went back and forth with Maverick about the foundation needed to increase open positions in small towns. I listened with half an ear. Maverick was doing exactly what he'd come to do, but I couldn't help but feel like he was intentionally pushing me out. Instead of discussing his thoughts with me and going over some of the data we needed to accumulate, he was doing it all himself.

I was no longer the youngest brother who got irritated with his siblings and went to the city for the weekend to burn off his irritation. I was a grown-ass male, and I'd even found the female of my dreams. If I wanted to keep her, I had to get the rest of my shit straight.

CHAPTER 7

evi

THE MEAL WAS SERVED on Deacon's patio. Two large picnic tables had been pushed together, and his backyard was filled with talking and laughter, interspersed with the occasional cry from Hazel.

Maverick was seated on the opposite end, as far away as he could get from me. He'd been peppering Steel about law enforcement needs all morning. Peridot Falls had one officer, basically a Steel since Steel was the only law Silver Lake needed other than Deacon's authority, but the cop in Peridot Falls wasn't from the ruling family. Maverick must be thinking of expanding to two or three law enforcement officers.

It made sense. We wouldn't need to rely on the county sheriff's office. While one of their deputies was a wolf shifter, the others were human, and the reasons they got called to Peridot Falls were often for decidedly not-human problems. During those instances, Memphis and Maverick had to work overtime to keep our shifter-secret safe. So, yeah, expanding our local law enforcement would be beneficial.

And again, he'd blocked me out of the conversation.

Briony's understanding gaze swept over me. She'd been fighting the lure of getting dragged into her own pack's government, but she recognized that our roles were different. My place was helping my clan, and Maverick wasn't letting me fulfill my obligation.

I rose from the table, gathering my dishes and Briony's. "Since you so gracefully hosted, Deacon, Maverick and I can do the cleanup."

My brother's head whipped around, and he smothered the spark of dominance. I didn't sense the same tug-of-war between Deacon and Steel, and I wanted to know why Maverick felt the need to subtly display his authority over me.

"Come on, Maverick. Let's go do some dishes like the old days." I kept an edge in my voice, letting him know there was a reason I volunteered us.

He smiled, falling back on his charm, and handed Hazel to Steel. "Only the dangerous dragon shifters do dishes."

Deacon chuckled. "And the most clever have a dishwasher for large family gatherings. I appreciate the help, guys." He stayed sitting, as did Steel. They must sense that I had business with Maverick.

We piled into the kitchen with an armload of dirty dishes. I was depositing my items by the sink when Maverick dropped his with a clatter.

I winced, annoyed. "You might want to be careful with our host's shit."

"Look, I don't mind helping." The sandpaper roughness to his voice said he was upset at himself for not thinking of it first. "But you want to tell me what this is all about?"

I turned to him and drew up to my full height. He had to know I was serious. I wasn't a little kid fucking around anymore. "I was about to ask you the same thing. We both happen to be in another dragon shifter community, with the intent of helping our own people, but you're not including me in the conversation. We had the entire car ride to discuss any items we wanted to bring up with the Silvers."

"We also had a cat shifter in the car who isn't part of our clan."

She would be if I had any say. "We're working on it. But I need you to work with me. For fuck's sake, Maverick, I'm tired of having fuck all to do in Peridot Falls."

Maverick's brows drew together and his expression turned quizzical.

I nodded, answering his unspoken question of *you are?* "I put up with how you and Memphis treated me for most of my life. But I've gotta tell you, the last few years have been irritating as hell. You treat me like I'm ten, like there's no reason for me to be around. But newsflash, I can't do anything else. I'm a Peridot. I'm also a living being who wants to do something with his life. So it's a little aggravating when it's my own siblings standing in the way."

"How the hell are we in your way?" He sounded more bewildered than defensive.

"When was the last time you told me about a city council meeting?" My anger was on the rise but I kept my volume down. We were guests in Deacon and Ava's home, and I didn't wish to make the morning awkward for them. "And when I do show up to meetings, you give me shit about my weekend. Do I call you out in front of the council members about why you and Astra broke up *again*? Do I ask you about why you aren't mated when around other people?"

Maverick's jaw clenched. "I'm just giving you shit. We're brothers."

"You're throwing me under the bus, and I don't know why. It's that same attitude that prompted the council's insistence to terminate me when Brighton's stalker tracked me down."

"You led him right to our people. You shifted in front of a human."

Shame burned in my chest. "And I took responsibility. Which would've been easier if I'd had the support of my family in the first place. Then maybe the council members —four people who watched me grow up—would've thought there was more purpose for me than just killing me off over a problem Memphis had already taken care of. I'd like to think I'm more to you—and them—than an example."

Maverick's jaw worked. Concern weighed heavy in his gaze. The council's reflexive reaction to the fear the human caused had been directed at me. Memphis was the ruler; they couldn't lose her. Maverick was her twin, and the two were close. My siblings were the treasures of Peridot Falls, and I'd been nothing. Was my reality finally sinking into him?

"I'm willing to do my part," I said. "But I need you to work with me."

Maverick stared at me for a moment, his jaw hard. Then he pinched the bridge of his nose, squeezing his eyes shut. "All right. I'm sorry. I get it. I still treat you like my little brother, like we're teenagers, but you're a grown male." His jaw worked as he stared out the window.

Everyone was still sitting at the table, chatting and laughing. "You're even going to get mated before me."

"I wouldn't be so sure. The last thing that girl out there wants is to be a cat shifter in a dragon community. She's put up with so much shit from her own pack, I need to make her see that living with me is worth more headache."

"She's going to have to prove herself, no matter where she goes."

Unless it was a big, human city. It'd be nice if dragon shifters were more welcoming of other shifter mates, and maybe they would be if I wasn't a Peridot. But I was, and the talk about Briony would spread. She might get challenged. I had no doubt. "I've only known her for a few days. It's a stretch to claim we're going to be mated."

"You don't see the way she looks at you." He pushed a hand through his hair and a hunk flopped on his head. He didn't immediately finger-comb it back into place.

"What's going on? Why did you really go to Jade Hills? Did you need a vacation?" Even if he did, I wanted to know what pressure was on him. He wasn't the ruler of our clan, but he had a lot of responsibility. Still, Maverick could handle whatever that job threw at him.

He ground his teeth together before saying, "Astra is getting mated."

I rocked back on my heels. "Whoa."

"Yeah." His expression was bleak. "Whoa."

"Who?"

"Jack Clarence."

Jack Clarence was a solid ten years older than me and several years older than Maverick and Astra. He was a quiet male who lived on the edge of town. He should've mated years ago, but he'd been stable and Memphis had kept a close eye on him. "Is she saving him?"

"Fuck if I know." Maverick shook his head and hooked

a hand on his hip while anchoring his other hand to the counter like he needed to steady himself. "We've been a thing for almost fifteen years. I just thought we'd end up together."

Maverick had less than five years until his milestone birthday. The entire town probably assumed the same thing I did—he and Astra had had plenty of time before the deadline. Typical Maverick and Astra drama. "When?"

"It's probably already done," he croaked.

"Shit," I breathed. Now his mood made sense. I liked Astra well enough, but she'd been a part of my life since I was a kid. Not quite like a sister, but like that family friend you were never sure what to think about. She could burn hot and cold, and I suspected she thrived on the tension between her and Maverick. Sometimes I wondered if that was all she knew, having been with Maverick since they were teens.

"So if I'm a bit of a bastard this week, I guess that's why."

"You'll find someone. Someone that treats you right."

He pushed off the counter and threaded both hands through his hair, fiddling with the strands until they were perfect. He was coming back online. "I've been thinking about that. What if... What if I don't know how to treat someone right? Astra and I were just... Toxic."

Pain laced his voice. The weight of all the years with his ex hung off of him, creating an aura of anxiety. I could almost hear the question echoing around his brain. *What if Astra found true happiness because I was the toxic one?*

"You're a good guy, Mav."

He gave me a droll look. "The ex who could only stand me for short lengths of time over two decades gets mated this week and you pull me aside in front of the leaders of all shifter kind to tell me I'm being a jackass."

"I didn't say your ego's not the size of your—"

"Giant, by the way. My ego's humongous." He cocked a brow, a clear signal we were moving past the heavy parts of our conversation.

"Maybe it's not, and that's why Astra left."

Maverick made a choking sound and his eyes bulged.

"Too soon?" I asked, sensing the frustrated rage rolling off him in waves.

"Way too damn soon, Levi." He dropped his chin and snorted. "But good one, fucker."

Briony

I THOUGHT I was stuffed after the ham and eggs and fresh veggie breakfast Deacon served us. But after a walk through the trails around the lake the town was named after, and much of downtown Silver Lake, my stomach rumbled while walking beside Levi up and down Main Street.

His bright gaze captured mine. "Let's stop at the café."

"We don't have to right now, if you're not hungry."

"I can always eat." He didn't look away, and his tone was aloof enough to tell me his statement had more than one meaning.

Heat crept up my neck, and I attempted to rescue myself by bringing up the pan of bars he had eaten. "I've seen your appetite in action."

"That was barely a hint, Briony."

"Are you two actually hungry," Maverick said, "or are we talking about fucking, because I'm an old man and I can't always tell."

I sputtered, flailing for a response, but Levi only grinned, his gaze dipping down to where my breasts pressed against my shirt, then farther to my bare legs. "Both."

"It's going to be a long few days," Maverick muttered before he veered to the left to jog across the street toward the café.

We followed and got enveloped in greasy, savory smells as soon as we entered. Maverick beelined toward a booth in the corner and sat smack-dab in the middle, sprawling his arms out to each side.

"Guess we're sitting next to each other." I slid into the booth closest to the window, and Levi sat beside me.

An older female appeared at the end of the booth. She didn't bother with a notepad, instead propping her hands on her hips. She peered at us like she was looking over readers but there were no glasses on her face. "What can I get you?"

Maverick ordered first. "Two hamburgers, nothing on them."

She gave a firm nod and looked at me and Levi.

"Same for me," Levi said.

"Do you have coconut cream pie?" I asked.

Another firm nod. "How many pieces you want?"

I was about to tell her just one, but I caught the spark of interest on Maverick's face and the little shrug of Levi's shoulder. They weren't going to order their own dessert, and no way in hell were they going to decimate mine like the chocolate cherry bars. "Bring three and a few extra forks."

She smirked and walked away.

The corner of Maverick's mouth lifted, and he speared Levi with a mirthful gaze. "Sounds like she knows you're after her cream pie."

"I've been after her sweets for a while," Levi answered.

I should welcome this more than Maverick's grumpy mood this morning, but my traitorous face blushed anyway. "I don't know what his tastes are," I muttered, hating how close to my insecurity I landed. Even after last night, I was still insecure about what he saw in me.

"From what I've heard," Maverick drawled, "whatever has to do with you. I've never seen Levi order pie in my life."

"Well, he was stuck on his sweet coffees before he met me." I wasn't continuing the conversation out of some search for validation. I liked this teasing side of Maverick, but I also wanted to learn more about Levi from his eyes. When the two disappeared into the house to talk, I worried that would be it for our trip, that the two would argue and insist on going their separate ways. Of course, I would've stayed with Levi, but it was clear how much he cared for his family.

"Yeah, man," Maverick said, "I didn't know you even liked coffee."

Levi rolled a shoulder. "Neither did I. But we don't have anything but gas station and diner coffee in Peridot Falls, and I wasn't exactly in the city at peak coffee-drinking hours."

Maverick's gaze jumped to me, then back to his brother. Was he surprised Levi talked so openly about his clubbing days around me? As if most adult, unmated shifters weren't highly sexual beings. I wasn't an exception either, I just made do with less.

"What else don't I know about you?" Maverick asked. His arms were still draped across the back of the booth, but his muscles were taut, like he was afraid of the answer.

"I did well in school and it wasn't because I cheated or girls helped me study." As Levi talked, I grew as still as

Maverick, hoping he'd continue. "I'm really bored at home. My motivation to go to Minneapolis every weekend wasn't to fuck, believe it or not. It was cool to talk to people who were doing stuff, moving forward in life. Listen to their plans and how they want to help others and their community. Then I'd go home and..."

"You'd come and have no support," Maverick grunted. "To be fair, we almost don't have enough people to support anything." His gaze flicked to me and back to Levi. Only this time, his look was loaded, almost like he was trying to send a message without saying words.

"What?" I asked.

Maverick smothered his grimace, but I caught his discomfort. "I was just thinking what a pivotal change it would be if you agreed to mate Levi and move to Peridot Falls."

I finished the rest for him. "A cat shifter moves to a town that's been highly discouraging to non–dragon shifters and it opens the floodgates to new arrivals?"

"Something like that."

"She's not a guinea pig," Levi said, his tone hard. Was he afraid the more his brother pushed the subject, the farther I'd want to get away from their hometown?

The temptation was there, but I earned enough hostility from my own pack of shifters, and I didn't want to encounter any with an entire clan of dragon shifters.

"But she kind of is," Maverick argued. "Anyway, attitudes are changing. Ronan Jade is now a Garnet member. You're friends with Brighton Garnet. Technology has given us the ability to be less isolated. People can live in small clans like Peridot Falls and have lucrative careers online. Attitudes are changing. No one wants to make the first move mating a cat shifter only to fear the council will be assholes."

"The council can be old-fashioned," Levi said.

"Because they don't know anything else. People are lonely, and they're leaving Peridot Falls to meet others. You can show them that it's possible to find someone and be happy in our little clan." He shook his head. "The pride of the past generation is fading. People hold on tight to their beliefs until they look around and their only choices for mates are various cousins."

I was in the middle of swallowing a mouthful of water. I sputtered, valiantly attempting to keep my mouthful from spewing across the booth. I mostly succeeded. Levi shook his head and handed a napkin to me. He rubbed my back while I finished coughing.

The waitress appeared and slid three plates of pie across the table. "Have some pie. It's good for the throat."

Levi continued stroking firm circles over my back. "Try not to drown her next time, will you?"

Maverick's expression turned grumpy like this morning. "Someone's gotta say it. I wish Memphis was dating, but she's going to push her thirty-five-year limit."

"She doesn't want to go outside of town to find a mate?" I asked with a partial wheeze. We had several cousins in town, but there were still single males.

He shrugged. "After that asshole years ago broke her heart, she's just not interested. I'm almost worried she'll dig her heels in about finding a partner. Find a friend. Hell, get a Jack Clarence like Astra did," he finished bitterly.

"With you and Memphis taking so long to find mates," Levi said, "it sets an example for the rest of the town."

"Why is that?" I asked. "Aren't you both flirting with death?"

"Soon enough, it will be," Maverick answered. "But then guys like Jack Clarence land a hot female like Astra and others think they can risk the delay too. We've got to expand our population, or it'll only be a few more generations before Peridot dies out."

An entire clan perishing seemed extreme. The dragon shifter population was never meant to be large, but it would be a shame for any clan to be lost. Silver clan governed all shifter kind, but the other clans took control of the packs nearest to them. Fewer dragon shifters meant more arguments among each sort of shifter.

Pressure settled on my shoulders that had nothing to do with the weight of Levi's hand. He'd stopped rubbing my back, but he kept his hand draped across the back of the booth. I liked having his arm around me, but this conversation was bringing up unspoken obligations.

"I'm starting to feel a bit like a broodmare," I admitted.

Levi's arm tensed behind me. "I assure you that's not how we view new mates coming into Peridot Falls. We're just assuming procreation is a natural result of increased mating."

Maverick sat forward, more serious than I'd seen him this entire time. "Absolutely. We're trying to make the town a better place, and if you don't feel safe, or like you have a reason to be there, then we're failing. I didn't see it before, but thanks to my annoying little brother, I do now."

I wanted to lighten the conversation. To return to discussions about coffee and food. "He can be kind of annoying."

"You didn't say that the other night," Levi growled.

I gasped, but Maverick's laugh dispelled my growing uneasiness. Until he said, "It won't take us long to visit the rest of the little communities around here. Come to Peridot Falls. We don't have a motel, but I know a guy you can stay with." His eyes twinkled, but the pie turned into a hunk of concrete in front of me.

"I..." What if I hated it and had the confirmation I

needed that it'd never work? What if I loved it and Levi's clan hated me?

Levi squeezed my shoulder. "Just think about it. All you have to do right now is enjoy your dessert."

That wasn't quite true. I was going to have to admit that I might go with Levi, love it, be welcomed, and then I'd leave Cougarton and be done with secrets. Be done with my history there. And ultimately, I didn't feel like I earned a life free from the secret of what I'd done.

CHAPTER 8

Levi

BRIONY HAD BEEN quiet much of the day. Most people wouldn't notice a change, Maverick was likely clueless, but I did. After our talk in the diner, she'd been reserved. In the businesses we frequented, the new bakery in Silver Lake, the ceramics shop based out of a shifter's home, and a small spa, she'd asked pertinent questions. She'd talk to the owners and managers, often beating Maverick to questions such as *How was business? Did they find the city council helpful when problems arose? How much were the ruling families involved?*

All inquiries she'd made with the utmost curiosity. People wanted to talk to her; they were open with her. Maverick had a lot of charisma, but the Peridot last name gave people pause. No matter how likable he tried to be, there were years of gossip and speculation about us. But Briony was an unknown. Her expression was open and her enthusiasm was genuine. She hadn't been this open in Cougarton.

Everyone we had talked to were dragon shifters, and a couple of human mates, but Briony had seemed to be in her element. Still willing to help us improve our town while pondering whether she wanted to be a part of it. She hadn't admitted to the latter but the coincidence of her coolness toward me did it for her.

"Time to head back?" Maverick asked.

The trip to Jade Hills would only take half an hour. There was no rush, but the day was growing late and we'd already stuffed ourselves with enough food to keep us sated for the rest of the day but also enough caffeine to keep us awake for several more hours. Our metabolism could burn the stimulant off quick enough, but it would have to compensate for the three extra servings I had.

We piled out of the drugstore I would've passed over if Briony hadn't spotted homemade taffy in the window. She carried a big bag full of three smaller baggies inside. She had chosen taffy flavors for Lachlan and Indy, another for her gran, and one just for her.

"It should be late enough that Lachlan and Indy won't feel they have to entertain us." Briony shoved her sunglasses onto her face. The black frames with a hint of teal in the color only reminded me of the eyes she had behind them.

"I'm ready if you are." We piled into my car. Briony in the passenger seat next to me and Maverick in the back.

My brother sprawled across the back seat and chatted about the businesses we'd been to and the information she'd gathered. Briony reviewed her taffy purchase before stroking her fingers over the ceramic mug she'd purchased. The piece was a dusky cream deepening to a rich brown at the base with purple and yellow wildflowers etched over the surface. She trailed her fingers over the designs. Was she really into her cup or that intent on ignoring me?

All the way back to Lachlan and Indy's, I talked with my brother and kept my mind on work. I didn't technically have a job, but after seeing how other shifter communities were thriving, I couldn't wait to dive into something that would help my people.

I pulled up to the two-story house, parking on the concrete slab in front of the garage. Maverick pushed open his door.

I stayed where I was and put my hand on Briony's arm just as her fingers landed on the door handle. "Hey, Mav. I've gotta talk to Briony for a couple of minutes."

When his gaze met mine, his bright irises were full of understanding. So it hadn't been my imagination. Briony had closed off from me. Maverick shut the door, and I was alone with her.

"Want to talk about it?" I asked, keeping my fingers on her warm, satiny skin.

Her gaze landed on where I was touching her and a beat of yearning passed through her eyes. "It's all moving so fast." She glanced out the passenger window.

I hadn't expected her to open up to me at all. Remaining quiet, I hoped she would continue talking. This thing between us was unconventional and there were still the issues we'd already discussed. "It's hard to believe it's only been a few days. I feel like I've known you for years."

She twisted in her seat to meet my gaze and slipped her hand into mine. "I really like you, Levi. I like your steady nature. I admire your loyalty to your people. And in this little bubble we're in right now, I can't think of anything more I want to do than try this thing out."

"But our talk at the diner has you spooked."

Her brow furrowed and she ran her lower lip between

her teeth. "Yeah, I guess. All the other concerns are still there but talk of repopulating the town added more."

"I'm not going to pressure you to fill your belly with a baby as soon as possible, Briony." The image of her, round with my child, hit me hard in the gut and ignited a flash of heat shooting straight toward my dick. The primal male inside me wouldn't hesitate to plant my seed deep inside of her and grow our family. But I was also a modern guy, and older than Briony. If she wanted to wait to have kids, then I had no issues.

And to think we're already discussing the idea of family and children so soon after we met told me the chemistry between us was real. I'd never considered settling down with anyone I'd been with before her.

"*You* might not," she said, "but what happens when I go into heat and suddenly I don't care about condoms? Heat has a way of changing minds—in the moment, and our first time together, we didn't pause to consider it at all."

I trailed the fingers of my free hand over the back of hers. Her anxiety was valid, but a part of me wondered how much was an excuse. "I wouldn't change my mind because I know how you feel. I'm not forcing you to be with me, Briony. I want to be with you. I want to be inside of you. I want to come home to you—or have you come home to me, I don't fucking care. But if you're not in it, if you're not happy, if you're not comfortable, then neither am I. And..." Another fact weighed on my mind, an option, but I didn't want to rush her. "I have to live in a dragon shifter community, Briony. It doesn't have to be Peridot Falls. It doesn't have to be hours away from Cougarton. Would you rather live in Jade Hills? Silver Lake? We have options, Briony, and I think you've been set on only one option for so long. You're afraid of being stuck, but you already are."

She let out a heavy sigh and was quiet for several moments. "You'd do that for me?"

"What we have doesn't happen every day. Sure, I'd love to be around my brother and sister. I'd rather dedicate my efforts to the community I grew up in, but in the end, I have to take care of my mate."

"I wish I deserved it."

"Why don't you think you do?"

She ran her lower lip through her teeth. "Because I'm as much a coward as I am a fighter and I worry that if you find out, that'll be the end."

"We're all like that."

"Not like me. A long time ago, I did something that wasn't brave, and I kept it quiet because I was afraid of making everything worse. That others would get hurt because of my impulsiveness. I haven't been the same since."

Was that why our lack of consideration in regard to protection bothered her? She was impulsive once, and it changed her life? "I hope someday you'll trust me with the story, but our past mistakes make us stronger in the future."

"Doesn't feel like it," she muttered. "I feel more scared than ever."

"Yet, you're here. You could've moved to a city anytime. You didn't have to go home after college. Yet, you didn't abandon your grandma. You came with me to Jade Hills, and I know you're going to say you had to leave, but you didn't have to leave with me. Feeling scared doesn't define you."

After a few moments of silence, she said, "I feel stronger with you."

Putting my fingers under her chin, I gently lifted her face so my gaze could capture hers. "No matter what goes on around us, I always come back here. You and I. What's between us is special, and we can't let anyone else ruin it."

"Including me?"

"Especially you."

"I'll tell you what happened. Someday. I need time to see what happened through an adult's eyes. But..." She squeezed my thigh and smiled. "Thank you for being patient, even if it's only been a few days."

Her gaze touched on the house, like she was overly aware that people were inside. They wanted to hear about our day, our insights, and where we were going next.

"You don't have to go to Peridot Falls."

"I'd like to. Hearing you and Maverick talk about your home made it more real."

"I happen to have a nice place. With a big bed."

She chuckled. "No guest room." Shaking her head, she grinned. "A big bed sounds a lot better than a rocky shore."

"Then come. Stay with me. You can leave whenever you want."

Uncertainty entered her gaze. "You drove."

"Take the car. I can always get another."

"Just like that?"

"I have a hoard, baby." I leaned close and lowered my voice. "Want to see it?"

"Hmm, I would like to get a closer look at your jewels." She bit her lip again. "You think I'll really get welcomed? Or will I get challenged?"

"We can't know until we arrive. Both, maybe?"

Her gaze swept the house then she adopted a faraway look in the direction of town. "I guess before I got to know you, and spent the day with you and your brother, and met all these other levelheaded rulers, I thought dragon shifters were naturally more aggressive and argumentative."

It was a natural assumption to make. We were larger,

we were in charge, and we all had egos the size of our beasts. But those were also the same reasons we were less confrontational. "With our size, we can't afford to let our tempers pop off like a bottle rocket, exploding high in the sky and landing wherever. Sometimes the embers land and reignite, causing a fire. We live too close to humans to risk that level of exposure. Two mountain lions or wolves fighting is a lot different than two dragons fighting."

Understanding lit her eyes and a small smile curved her pretty pink lips. "You sound as if you had that lecture before."

"We all have."

"It makes sense, just like it makes sense that other shifters don't grow up knowing the same about dragons. It keeps us wary of you. We keep our distance."

"I don't want you to keep your distance, Briony. I don't want any space between us. And after everyone goes to sleep, I'd like you to meet me back at the lake, and I'd like to burn through the box of condoms I just bought."

Sexiness edged her grin. "Then I suppose we should go in and update everyone on our day." She dropped her volume to a sultry whisper. "So you can show me just how many condoms you can burn through at a time."

Briony

THE LAST COUPLE OF DAYS, Levi, Maverick, and I had to work in three small towns. One was Wildrose outside of Silver Lake, and from there we had gone to Gemstone to visit the Emerald clan, and yesterday we'd spent the day in a mixed shifter community close to the border.

Wildrose had a mostly human population, but thanks to its proximity to Silver Lake, a few dragon shifters were able to live and work in and around the town. Levi had known the rulers of Gemstone, and we had lunch with them so Maverick could get to know the ruling family as well. They had three kids, but we hadn't been able to meet them.

Now, we were in Minnesota, almost to Peridot Falls. Maverick was following us in his car. My stomach was a mess. I'd eaten the breakfast of eggs and hash browns Lachlan and Indy had made us, and I should be ravenous for lunch. Instead, I worried I'd hurl scrambled eggs all over the dashboard. Food poisoning or nerves?

Levi drove with an arm draped over the wheel. "I'm gonna pull into the rest stop up ahead."

Who was I kidding? Absolutely, it was nerves. I teetered on a precipice and I was leaning more toward one side.

I had my suitcase full of clothing and the trinkets I had bought over the last few days in the trunk. I had a bag of taffy for Gran, a coffee mug for Uncle Lewis, and a bottle of chokecherry syrup for my cousin. I wasn't sure if they were parting gifts or tokens of my appreciation, or both. Gran had rallied around me, and my uncle and cousin weren't necessarily close to me, but they were still family. They had done what they did to protect me, thinking I was weaker than those who would challenge me. Maybe I couldn't take on DJ, but I was confident enough in my abilities. I wished I could tell them why I was so cautious, but years of silence made it harder to talk.

The drive was going way too fast, and I was grateful for the stop. Levi would be turning off the interstate soon. I watched in the mirror for Maverick. He continued past the off-ramp in his car.

There were a few other cars and semis in the parking

lot. I got out and stretched my arms high above my head. I started walking and Levi wandered next to me. It was nice to just be with him. After the last two nights of meeting at the lake and getting lost in each other's bodies, I was more comfortable around him than ever. After we'd explored each other and had sex, we had lounged on the beach and talked. He had told me stories about growing up with Memphis and Maverick, and how he used to misbehave to get the attention of his older siblings. He'd admitted he was the spoiled surprise baby. Young enough that his parents had let him get away with everything just shy of murder.

I wasn't much different. Instead of acting out, I had closed up on myself, but my family had allowed it. I was the only child of Gran's daughter, and my mother had been taken from us so ruthlessly.

Gran had been distraught. Like a caged lion, she'd prowled through town, harassing anyone she thought was tied to Mom's death. And like everyone else, she had assumed Ree's aunt was guilty since she'd also disappeared the same night. But without proof, she couldn't retaliate. She couldn't start an inner pack war without irrefutable proof—and that proof would stay hidden and keep the pack from tearing itself apart.

I tipped my face to the sun to keep the bad memories at bay. "So Memphis isn't like Maverick?" I was nervous about meeting her too. Was Maverick's charm used to make up for his abrasive sister? Gran could be difficult, but she was my gran. Memphis had no reason to like me.

Levi had told me many stories about her, but he hadn't spoken much about present-day Memphis. From the pictures I'd seen of her online, she looked edgy. Same dark hair. Shrewd eyes and a challenging expression.

Levi stuffed his hands in his pockets. "Memphis isn't

Maverick's opposite per se, but it's like they're switched around."

"So your brother puts on a happy face for the crowd?"

"And Memphis gives them attitude. It's effective."

I squinted up at him, loving how the bright summer light highlighted the edges and planes of his face from his high cheekbones to his sharp nose. "How do you mean?"

He thought for a moment. "People behave differently around them. Memphis isn't afraid to speak her mind, so they censor their speech around her to avoid getting their head bitten off."

"Is it an act?"

He chuckled and I wanted to lean my head on his chest and let the sound rumble through my cheek. "It's not completely an act. Depending on her mood, she may very well do some head ripping. And Maverick always seems to be in a good mood, so people are more open with him than they would be with my sister about complaints and problems. Yet they're more likely to tell Memphis a lot of good things, like they're hoping to improve her disposition."

"And they can come together and share information. Good arrangement." And I could see how it left Levi on the outs. "You said your house is on the edge of town?"

A shadow crossed his face, and I stopped. Did he want to bring me to his home? I couldn't think of another reason why he wouldn't talk about it.

He stopped and faced me, his gaze sweeping around us. Cars were flowing in and out of the rest area, but we stood alone at the edge of the sidewalk by the on-ramp. "My place is on the very edge of town, and I haven't been home since I was kicked out."

"But you've been gone for weeks."

"Months."

He lived on the edge of town, and he'd come home late after spending a night in the city. I saw it all play out in my head, piecing together the information he told me during our time together. He'd thought he was alone, and he shifted. The human saw him, and the rest is history.

"I'm glad Memphis killed the bastard."

Surprise lifted his brows. "I didn't realize you were so cutthroat." There was humor in his tone, but also curiosity.

I worked hard not to reveal that side of myself. "I can be, when the occasion calls for it. I try to avoid those instances—that's the difference."

We started wandering back toward the car. I was more relaxed than I had been. He must've sensed my nerves firing up until they were roaring at full blast.

"Thanks for stopping," I said as we got into the vehicle.

He tucked my hand into his. "I want you to be comfortable in my home. Anything you need."

"I need you to keep being you."

His eyes glittered, and heat infused my body. If we weren't in public, we'd steam up the windows of the car. After several miles, he turned off the highway. Trees started crowding the road and towns got fewer and farther between.

Was this my new home? Would there be trouble? Was I willing to sink my claws into someone just because they thought I wasn't good enough for Levi?

All those answers waited ahead for us.

CHAPTER 9

evi

I TOOK the back roads to my place. Narrow, worn gravel paths with clumps of grass growing between the wheel divots. They were hell on the car, but I had a pickup in the garage at my house.

Briony had been peering out the windows the whole trip. "I'm glad we came here first."

Town could wait. The dragon in me, the male who wanted to mate and settle down, wanted her to see my place. I wanted her to start thinking about it as our place. I wanted her cinnamon-sugar scent to soak into my walls and furniture until my house was as much hers as mine. I was getting way ahead of myself but I was crazy about this girl.

Later, she'd meet Memphis. The last of my close family. Briony had done fine around Maverick, but Memphis was more of a wild card. My sister cared about me, and she strove to be a strong leader. Would those two principles clash over Briony? Memphis had saved my ass when the council called for my punishment, and she had urged me to at least meet Briony. But if members of the clan decided not to like my hopefully future mate, then what?

Only time would tell, and I wanted Briony to myself for a while longer. "I'm glad you don't mind. You're not the only one who needed a breather before braving everyone else." When she blinked at me, I gave her a sheepish smile. "I admit to being nervous too. I just want to be around you without the rest of the bullshit a little longer."

"You don't want to go get milk and get challenged?"

"That seems to happen around you."

"Once. Twice," she amended when I arched a brow. "And yes, the only two times you were out with me in Cougarton, but to be fair, Sasha and Ree didn't challenge me. They alluded to it."

"They would've, if you had stayed in Cougarton."

"Totally."

I should've left it at that, but I felt the need to remind her. "There's no such thing as anonymity in Peridot Falls. Word is going to spread that you're here. I doubt DJ or the two females will track you into dragon shifter territory, but they likely know you're here."

The sunlight shining through the leaves and into the car made her eyes shine. "I'm aware. They're going to talk shit. They might feel like they can't reach me, but I don't know that it'll stop them from trying to mess with me."

"You can mess back."

She gave a noncommittal shrug.

I turned down the drive that would take us to my house. She leaned forward, her lips parting when she got a good view of my place. My home was nothing spectacular, but it was cozy, charming and mine.

I hadn't gone full log cabin, but utilized a lot of rock and big windows. If an unsuspecting human stumbled onto my property, they would think it would make a nice hunting spot. Big enough for a few people, but buried too far in the rural woods to be useful.

"This place is gorgeous." Her reaction stroked my ego.

It was the dragon shifter in me. I wanted to give the female I wished to be my mate pretty bobbles, and that included a home and a valuable hoard. Some of the jewels from the hoard I'd inherited went into buying the house. I fixed it up during my downtime and fielded criticisms about not hiring out and providing jobs for someone local. But a guy needed to have something to do. Was I supposed to sit on the porch and watch the grasshoppers jump around while someone else did all the work?

"Thanks. It was a bit of a fixer-upper, but the foundation and structure were solid." I sounded nonchalant, but I oozed with pride. As much as I wanted to bring commerce to town and create jobs, I was glad I had done this myself.

While she got out of the car, I went to the trunk and hauled her bags out. Her impressed gaze stayed on my home while I carried her luggage behind her, smiling to myself.

"It smells so fresh." Her grin was sheepish. "It's not that Cougarton stinks, but in town, there is still the faint scent of exhaust and of course the burger smell from the restaurants downtown."

"I get what you mean. It's like being at Lachlan and Indy's versus being at the coffee shop."

"Except no smell of coffee."

"I can change that. Wait till you see what I have in the kitchen."

With a giggle, she entered my home and gazed all around her while finding her way to the kitchen. I set her bags by the bottom of the stairs and followed her while she explored.

When we finally arrived in the kitchen, she stopped and stared at the silver espresso machine on the countertop. "I don't even know what that is, but I think it has something to do with coffee."

"I can make my own caramel macchiatos."

"You're a man of many talents."

I crowded her toward the small square island in the middle of the floor. With a grin, she backed up.

"I can show you one of those talents right now."

The flush was back in her cheeks. The female couldn't hide her desire. It darkened the yellow flecks in her irises and made her breaths quicken. "You're going to make me a cup of coffee?" Humor danced in her tone.

My predatory stalking had nothing to do with the drink, unless it included my mouth on hers, getting my fill. "Oh, I'm going to take a nice, long gulp of something sweet."

I was tempted to drop to my knees and roll down her shorts and underwear as I went. But she'd been chewing on the licorice taffy she'd bought in Silver Lake. I didn't mind the licorice flavor, but I had a feeling I would become addicted to the taste of it on her lips.

Bending, I captured her mouth with mine and swept my tongue inside her mouth. Perfect. Just as I thought. The spicy zing of licorice and the deceptively innocent flavor of Briony. Groaning, I deepened the kiss as she wrapped her arms around my shoulders.

Maybe we weren't going to make it into town at all

today. I had Briony in my house, at my mercy. I had just swept my hand up her shirt and was stroking the flesh of her abdomen when my front door slammed.

Jerking back, I nearly ripped her shirt off to twist around and find out who the intruder was. A startled gasp left Briony, but she didn't hide behind me. There was more steel in this little cat shifter than most people realized. I understood why she hid it, and the longer I was around her, the more I respected her control.

Memphis swaggered around the corner, her Keen brand rubber-sole sandals smacking on the hardwood floor. She pushed her aviator sunglasses into her jet-black hair.

"What are you doing here?" I sounded hostile, but only because I was an aroused shifter who'd been minutes away from sinking into the wet heat of the female I was crazy about.

Memphis's dark brows lifted, and she regarded me and Briony, her gaze lingering on Briony's shortened breaths and then shifting over to assess my aroused estate. "Maverick said you two are the real deal, but I kind of didn't believe it. I thought you were playing the game to get back to town."

No games. "And you're here because?"

The corner of her mouth tipped up. "There is nothing as satisfying to a sister as cockblocking her brothers."

I rolled my eyes, but I couldn't stop a chuckle escaping. I even heard a faint giggle coming from Briony. The tension drained out of the room as quickly as the blood left my erection.

She flipped her hair in a move that nearly dislodged her sunglasses. "Anyway, I hardly ever get to do it to you. It's my favorite pastime with Maverick."

"I wanted to show Briony my place."

The humor died from Memphis's eyes and she appraised us both. She was seeing right through me and it was a struggle not to fidget. "Eventually you have to bring her to town. In fact, why don't we meet for supper at Honor's so I can officially welcome her."

It wasn't a question.

"Is that a good place to go over our notes with you?" Briony said in a calm voice, as if Memphis didn't intimidate her in the slightest. On the outside, Briony appeared unruffled, her expression curious but impassive. But there was a tautness in her muscles that wasn't there when I had her backed up to the island, ready to ravish her.

Confusion lifted Memphis's brows. "Notes?"

"Maverick told you what we've been doing the last few days, right?" I asked.

"He said you guys have come up with ideas for Peridot Falls." She gave her head a little shake. "Yeah, I'll listen to any insights you have, but I hope it includes how to get others here and grow the town. We've only got a few hundred people—no spare bodies to work bakeries and coffee shops and candy shops." Her tone indicated she thought none of those types of businesses were important. "And if we don't have people to work them, we definitely don't have people to frequent them."

"That was a concern in some of the places we visited," Briony said. "But they found once they opened their doors, the people came. Lacey at the coffee shop in Jade Hills said the research she'd done highlighted a commonality with coffee shops—they aren't necessarily direct competition. There just seem to be enough customers for each one that opens. There's only gas station to-go coffee in town."

As long as we were talking about this, and my sister wasn't shutting Briony down, I continued. "Instead of making their beverages at home, they can go out to buy them. It's a treat that becomes a habit that almost turns into a necessity."

Briony nodded enthusiastically. "I think a bakery would be the same. Instead of doing everything themselves, at home, a lot of residents will happily purchase what they need. It's a treat, but it also takes another task off their plate."

Memphis crossed her arms and kicked a hip out. Her expression remained dubious, but I detected a hint of curiosity deep in her eyes. "Sounds like you put more thought into it than just sampling donuts all over the place."

"I also drank a lot of caramel macchiatos," I said glibly. Of course, my sister assumed I fucked around for the last few months.

Briony's fingers curved around my biceps, and she hugged close to me. "Levi has a lot of great insight. He's been thinking about this for a while, and it's been really fun to hear his enthusiasm for building up Peridot Falls."

Her words were pointed, genuine, and the sentiment wasn't missed by Memphis. My sister's brows ticked up. "Would it surprise you if Maverick said something similar?"

"I've had a talk with Maverick about my role in town. You and I should probably do the same." I wasn't usually so forthright with Memphis unless I was teasing her, but I couldn't return home and be the same guy who'd left. My time away was meant to benefit the town by way of improving me. I came home feeling like I had a purpose—because I did, dammit.

"We'll definitely do that." Memphis backed up and shoved her hands in the pockets of her jeans. "But your first hurdle is getting your mate accepted by the clan." When she reached the entryway to the kitchen that would lead to the front door she'd barged in, she stopped. "Just remember that while you have a role with the clan, it's not fighting her battles."

~

Briony

I SLIPPED my hand into Levi's. He parked on the street in front of a café. The sidewalks had been relatively quiet as he'd driven through town. Memphis's message had been clear. I needed to hold my own in this little town and she wouldn't tolerate hiding.

Chagrined to admit I'd been willing to hide for an undetermined amount of time, I agreed with her.

How was a cat shifter going to take on a dragon shifter? I would be less worried if I had the charisma of Maverick and the likability of Levi. But females who were less than accommodating didn't often get the benefit of the doubt.

I gripped Levi's hand, and he led me into the little café. The place wasn't any different than any other we had been in over the last few days. On the small side, the walls had been repainted an off-white, and the drop ceiling didn't add to the appeal. Older, well-used tables and chairs were scattered through the middle of the dining area and plain black booths lined the walls. The servers' area flanked the doors to the kitchen.

What made this café stand out were the paintings lining the walls. Cheerful watercolors as sophisticated as they were simple were hung side by side, almost as if on display in a fine art gallery. The arrangement didn't do the work justice. Each piece should have its own square footage on the wall with a special light highlighting the fine detail.

Levi towed me toward the booth Memphis was waiting in, her arms spread out on either side of her like Maverick had done. I barely noticed her as I tried to take in each of the paintings we passed. In one, the profile of a young woman stared into space in front of her. Her expression could've evoked a myriad of emotions—helplessness, curiosity, peace, uncertainty. Another was a setting, a blue-gray stream trickling over rocks with tall trees soaring on either side.

As I slid into the booth, I stared at the picture hanging above Memphis's head. It was an aerial view of the town, more like a dragon's-eye view. Each building lacked detail but was specific enough in size and coloring that I knew what each place was. A curlicue *H* was painted on the bottom of each photo. The artist's signature.

The server that appeared at the edge of the booth handed Memphis a menu and tossed the other two down between me and Levi. Startled, I glanced up. The dark-haired female was older than me but probably only around Levi's age. Her crystalline green eyes bored into me, then switched to Levi. Annoyance flickered in their bright depths, but I sensed a hint of amusement. Was she going to mess with us?

This was it. I didn't sense ill will from her, but that didn't mean I wouldn't get tested.

"Honor," Levi greeted, his tone cautious.

"Levi. Hear you've been busy."

He stretched an arm behind my shoulders, not quite a protective move but a way to stake his claim. "I try to keep it that way."

"It can be hard work to stay out of trouble." She lifted a shoulder. "Just like the difficulty in calling a girl back."

Levi tried to conceal his flinch, but I felt it more than I

observed it. His expression remained amicable. "It's tiring to hold a grudge."

"Oh, there are always ways to reignite it. Like showing up in town with a cat shifter on your arm. At least with all the humans, you didn't bring them back to Peridot Falls."

Memphis watched the interaction, an amused smile tilting the corners of her mouth upward.

I had been prepared to be the one challenged, but Honor apparently had unfinished business Levi had known nothing about. I might be considering mating him —that was a lie. I had failed at every attempt to talk myself out of mating him, and now I was in Peridot.

"You moved on quickly enough, Honor. How's Mads?"

"He doesn't purr."

It was my turn to flinch. A definite dig toward me. I met her challenging gaze but confusion swirled in my brain. Her words weren't insulting, just pointed, and I didn't sense hostility. What was her goal?

"I do admit to purring," I said. "But he's really got to earn it. I've never had a problem with him calling me back though. Since he just kind of showed up and never left."

Honor pressed her fingertips into the top of the table. "What are you saying? That what he and I had wasn't good enough to make him stick around?"

I caught the slight stench of irritation. Had she been messing with me, and I unintentionally insulted her? Dammit, I was no good at this. Yet at the same time, wasn't that the point? She tossed some shade my way, and I threw it back?

"I don't know the story, but I'm guessing this Mads stuck around?" When fondness flickered in her gaze, I continued. "I bet he even calls when you don't expect him to. Sounds like it worked out better for you."

She shifted her gaze to stare out the far window behind

us, as if talking about whoever Mads was to her had summoned him onto the street. Perhaps he worked in one of the buildings in the direction she was looking.

Her name and the *H* on the paintings clicked together. "You're the artist."

Her gaze jerked to me just like Levi's and Memphis's did. But my excitement built too fast to keep my mouth shut. I plowed forward.

I twisted in my seat and pointed to the painting of the woman staring into space. "That's you. Did you paint all of these?"

She recoiled, putting her hand on her chest. Dark curls billowed around her head where in the painting, they were pulled back. The profile wasn't defined and the eyes were darker, but those were easy ways to disguise the model. To have anonymity. Maybe as an artist, she didn't want people to tease her for painting herself.

"Yeah, I painted these." She shifted her stance and folded her hands in front of herself like she was suddenly awkward. I doubted it was my attention on her that did it.

Memphis said, focused on Honor. "Seriously? You're the one that's done all of these?"

Honor ducked her head, her earlier bravado gone.

"I knew you dabbled in painting," Levi said, "but it didn't dawn on me these were yours."

Honor rolled her eyes, but a smile touched her lips. "Because you've avoided me since we dated."

"Your mate gets a little rangy about me."

Honor lifted a shoulder like it was a nonissue. "I may have played it up. I like it when he gets all territorial."

Levi barked out a laugh, unconcerned about how a white lie could've gotten him into a fight. I was grateful there were no true hard feelings between them but far more interested in her work. "Do you sell them?"

Her smile faded. "No. I have a lot on my hands running this place." Her fingers danced over her still-flat belly. "And with the new one coming early next year, I don't know how much time I'll have to dabble."

"What if someone sold them for you?" I asked.

Memphis watched the entire conversation, not adding a word. Perhaps I should've broached the idea with her before I started gushing to Honor about it, but whether or not I stayed in Peridot Falls and Levi was allowed to bring in new businesses, Honor had to know there were possibilities if she was interested.

"My work is more of an escape," Honor said.

"That's cool too. Gotta have an outlet."

She tilted her head and inspected me. "You're not like the other cat shifters I've met."

"Half-feral and arrogant?" I smiled. "We're not all that way, but it's hard not to be intimidated around dragons."

She lifted her brows. "And you're not intimidated?"

"What kind of shifter would I be if I confessed?"

Memphis snickered, and Honor tossed her head back and laughed. There was movement at the other tables. People had been watching our reaction. I couldn't see them, but the air lightened. I could breathe easier.

Maybe I could do this. And if I could, that would only mean… I could make a life with Levi. One that included me among the people and not avoiding the crowd.

Levi

Briony visibly relaxed during our meal. She hadn't been the only one. Honor had been a test with Memphis as the proctor. Briony might've thought it was done, but we were at the bank now.

I held open the heavy glass door of the bank. United Falls was in an old brick building. The loan officer had been my prom date and the first girl I'd slept with. She was mated with two kids. The teller had changed my diapers when I was a kid. Shelby Noggins had been Mom's best friend growing up and she was the closest thing to an aunt my siblings and I had.

Two females who had close ties to me and likely wished me the best. My former prom date, Jackie, had dumped me as soon as she'd set eyes on her mate who'd been in town visiting family, but we'd remained good friends.

What was Memphis up to?

Heels clicked on the floor. Jackie dressed for the job and it didn't matter if she worked with the same families month after month. She wore charcoal slacks and an ivory blouse. Her mahogany hair was tied in a bouncy knot on top of her head. She was gorgeous but my pulse didn't jump when my gaze landed on her. My blood kept circulating like normal instead of rerouting to my dick like when I'd set eyes on Briony that first time. Like when I looked at her any time of the day.

"Memphis, hi." She grinned when she saw me and threw her arms out. "Hey, Levi."

I loosely returned her hug. "Jackie, it's been a while. How was your Alaskan vacation?"

She pulled away, her curious gaze taking in Briony for a moment. "So nice. Acres and acres of trees. It's crazy to think what trouble we could get into there in our dragon forms. I couldn't believe when we got home, and I heard about you. And then I heard more." She clasped her hands in front of her, her smile pleasant. "I see the cat shifter rumors are true. Or should I smell they're true?"

Briony's inhale was slow, measuring. So that was Memphis's angle. She was testing me. How much would I defend Briony? How would Briony handle all the females in my life who could act more than a touch territorial?

Briony stuck her hand out. "The cat shifter in question. I'm used to being talked about. And smelled."

Jackie tilted her head, making her bun jiggle. "And it doesn't bother you?"

"It's different than what I'm used to," Briony answered. "And so far, better."

Jackie exchanged a look with Memphis. "What draws you to our Levi?"

Briony's reply was simple. "His ass."

Jackie blinked, and Memphis coughed. Served them right.

"Just kidding," Briony said. "Sort of. It's what keeps me with him, among other body parts. He's a considerate male, and he makes me think I could have what my parents had before my mom died. No one else has ever made me consider."

I smelled Shelby's rose-petal scent before she rushed me, tossing her bony but strong arms around my neck. "Levi, I was so worried." She clapped me on the back hard enough to make me cough. "I thought you'd get snatched up by some other clan and have to stay there." When she abruptly released me, I almost stumbled back. She spun on Briony. "And when I heard about you!"

Only excitement rolled off Shelby. Jackie's lips quirked, and that was when I knew I shouldn't have worried. Memphis had been busy spreading the rumor of Briony and building support for me. She was still putting Briony through the motions of the test, as if it was a checkbox to tick off, but she wasn't worried.

Time for proper introductions. "Shelby, Jackie, this is

Briony Sanders from Cougarton. It's just over the Canadian border."

Briony shook their hands, her grip as strong as theirs and if she didn't wince when Shelby pumped her arm, then she had some hidden strength. Pride surged through me, and I realized I was grinning. This was going so damn well. I didn't know what could go wrong, but I had to believe this was meant to be. Our meeting might've been arranged, but we were meant to be together, as good as fated mates.

Look at me, all fucking romantic.

After greetings, I faced Memphis. "Did you bring her here so Jackie can spill all my awkward high school dating moves, or do we have business?"

Humor passed through her expression. "I thought Shelby could talk about how you used to dance naked in front of the picture window when you were two." She turned serious. "No. Maverick called me a couple days ago and told me what you two had been talking about and what you've been researching. I think securing financing from the bank would kill two birds with one stone."

As opposed to using my hoard. That made sense. The interest would go to the bank and filter down to the employees.

"Let's go into my office." Jackie started walking and speaking over her shoulder. The other employees, two males and three females, watched us, but she didn't lower her voice. Use the rumor mill to our advantage, just like Memphis had with Briony. "Shelby's been at the bank the longest and knows the town's history better than anyone, so Memphis asked her to be included. I've found some grants you may be interested in."

I grabbed Briony's hand. "Mind if I talk to Briony a moment before we huddle?"

I had an urgency I couldn't describe. I was getting

everything I'd wanted, but there was one thing I yearned for above the rest.

Memphis inclined her head and disappeared into a glass-walled office. I glanced around and tugged Briony toward the nook that housed the bathrooms. "You okay with this?"

"Getting flaunted around town to see how I'll react to potentially insulting comments from people who know you?" She shrugged. "It's been going well."

"No, not that." I pressed a kiss to the corner of her mouth. "But you've been amazing and yes, these people know me, and we're still friends after..."

She quirked a brow. "After you've had sex?"

"Not with Shelby. She's more like family. Both Jackie and Honor are happily mated now, but they care about me. I'm not concerned with what they think. I'm concerned about you more, and we're going into a meeting to talk about opening a business." Without knowing what business or where. "This town has gone from pushing away other shifters to welcoming you in when you haven't even confirmed you want to stay. I want you to stay. I want you to be with me, to be mine. But just like I wasn't going to force you, I'm not willing to trick you either. This meeting isn't meant to pressure—not from me anyway."

Her pink tongue wicked out to lick through the seam of her lips and I nearly groaned. How bad was it if I whisked her into the bathroom?

"The truth is... I already made my decision before coming here. But it scared me, and it was easier to play along." She slid her hands up my shoulders and around my neck. "I want to stay too, but I'd like to talk to you about some things first. About what happened with my mother."

I draped my hands on her arms. When I first met Briony, our chemistry was off the charts, but she was guarded. She still was, but slowly, she was letting me in. I didn't know what she had to discuss with me. I didn't know what more there was to her past or what had closed her off. But she was mine. She would be mine. "We'll talk. Right after I devour you when we get home."

"Promise?"

CHAPTER 10

evi

I LIVED up to my promise. I was usually the calm and collected one in meetings, the guy others thought didn't care. Today, I hadn't lived up to the reputation. I'd been engaged, shared my thoughts, but I'd propelled the discussion of loans, grants, and locations to warp speed.

I was back home now, and Briony was climbing out of the car. She squeaked as I hauled her over my shoulder and hip-checked the door closed.

She fisted the back of my shirt. "I can walk."

"I know. I like watching your ass when you do."

Her body shook with her laugh. "I thought you were going to drag me into the bedroom."

"I almost did." I set her on the top steps of the porch to my house. Her face was flushed and her hair was wild. The stress and the rigidity of her features from the first time I saw her in Cougarton were gone. She was happy and excited about our future together.

I stroked my fingers down her cheek. "I'm going to keep this smile on your face for the rest of your life."

"Is this officially you asking me to mate you?"

"I've asked."

She lifted a shoulder. "We've talked about it."

"Fuck, I want you, Briony. I want you to be mine. I want to run through these trees with you and chase that tail until I catch you and claim you under the stars."

I brushed my fingers down to her collarbone. "Speaking of claim..."

Her eyes dilated, and her lips parted. "You want to claim me?"

The claiming bite could be more intimate than the mating and it wasn't just because the couple had sex while claiming. Mating was the final closure of a relationship but it could be as much of a transaction as the couple wanted. An open relationship for mates who hadn't found their one but needed to adhere to the dragon shifter time line of mating. An obligation. A more official handshake.

The claiming bite was raw passion. A proclamation to everyone that this person belonged to another. It could go both ways, and maybe it would. Maybe Briony would sink her teeth into my neck and I'd wear her claim as proudly as I would a wedding band.

I leaned close and let my breath feather over her ear. "I'm going to sink my fangs into you while I'm buried deep between your legs and you're crying my name."

Her inhale was audible, and she brought her face closer to mine. "Promise?"

"You have my word."

Another little squeak. Dragons didn't make arbitrary promises. We didn't make vows we couldn't keep. To fail could mean death if the other party reported our lack of fulfillment.

Giving Briony my word was putting my life in her hands. Cat shifters might not share the same penchant for promises, but she held my life in her hands regardless.

"Levi, I think…" She wet her lips again, and I tracked her tongue like the ravenous male I was. "I think I keep falling more in love with you each day I know you."

A growl ripped out of me. This girl fell for a guy who dove into her life and wedged himself into her business. This girl fell for a guy who meant well but never actually contributed to his clan. This girl had faith in me, and I refused to give her up.

I surged forward, pushing her back until her back hit the floor of the porch. I was still between her legs, a couple of stairs down, but this position opened her nicely to me. I just had to get her clothing out of the way.

"I'm going to fuck you in broad daylight, Briony." And this wouldn't be the last time. "You are mine."

Another whimper left her, and she rolled her hips up. Enough waiting. We were both ready to move forward.

I yanked her shorts and underwear down. I'd prefer her naked, but raising her up to a seated position to get her top off would take too much time. My erection was pounding at the clasp of my pants. My future mate's scent surrounded me and I needed to feast. I hooked her legs over my shoulders and delved between her folds. She arched her back and buried her hands in my hair. I was grateful I didn't put the tie in today.

Her taste landed on my tongue and I forgot everything but how to make her come. She bucked under my mouth, my name leaving her lips and getting carried on the wind.

I barely threaded two fingers into her when she arched again, her muscles going tight, and heat exploding against my face. I growled into her, adding an extra rumble as she came.

"Levi!"

There were no others around, but satisfaction flowed through me hearing her shout my name, at my home, to echo across my land.

I crawled up her body and ripped my shirt over my head. "That was fucking beautiful."

She was still trying to catch her breath. She blinked from the overhang of the porch to me. A slow, sexy smile spread across her face. "I can't believe I came that fast." She shook her head. "No, never mind. I believe it with you—I just keep thinking I should last longer."

"I make it my job to know how long you want to last."

The smile turned dreamy. "I seem to be involved in all of your jobs."

"I wouldn't have it any other way." This connection was what I wanted. I grew up with siblings who had each other. I'd been envious they had a person. It'd change for them as they took mates, but as I got older and stayed alone, I wondered if I was destined to be as wandering in my love life as my personal life.

I was done soaring over the trees. I had a shifter to lead me through them. To keep my feet on the ground and live life. "I love you, Briony Sanders."

She cupped my face. "I love you too, Levi. Now put your bite on my neck."

I ripped my pants getting them open. I didn't feel the bite of the fabric in my skin as the seams tore. The relief of my cock being free took over. I kept her legs spread and plunged inside.

"God, yes, Levi," she groaned.

Her wet heat clamped around me, and I started thrusting immediately. I balanced myself on the steps, watching myself take her. Her sex glistened with her previous release and she coated me. Lightning raced down my spine and coiled in my balls, tightening them up. I wasn't going to last long. This moment was too momentous. Too important.

Bracing my legs, I lifted Briony while I still impaled her and held her to me. I wasn't going to bash her back into the floorboards while I drove into her and clamped down on her neck.

Twisting, I sat, letting her straddle me. She continued the motion, riding me, but I held her so tightly she could barely move. She didn't have to. The grip of her body was enough to drive me wild.

I yanked her shirt over her head, and she shook her hair off her neck. She was bared to me. I latched on to the spot, clenched my hold tighter, and brushed a kiss over the dip of her collarbone. She trembled in my arms but tipped her head to the side. I licked her skin, relished her shiver, and just as energy roared through my shaft, I bit down.

Her cry carried on the wind, my name traveling over my property and dissipating into the air. The force of my claim slammed her over her peak and her walls clamped around me. Her orgasm enhanced my own. The taste of her flesh was in my mouth. The indentations of my teeth would stay for a while, but I was careful not to cut through her skin. And once she was all healed, my claim would be left behind. Other shifters would know she was not only taken, but she was also wanted. Desired. Revered.

I stroked her sensitive skin with my tongue. She went limp in my arms, aftershocks rocking her body and echoing into me.

"That was..." She palpated the spot on her neck I'd bit. "Intense."

"Yeah, it was."

"Is it like a one-time thing or..."

"Wanna test it out and see?"

Briony

THREE DAYS HAD GONE by since I was claimed by my future mate. I didn't think I'd get this far with a male. Definitely not with a dragon shifter. And not living in a town with fewer people than even Cougarton. And I think I'd like it.

There wasn't much to get out and do in Peridot Falls. I could see why Levi had been listless. I was bored. We'd met with Jackie again. Toured the empty building on the edge of town. It was two stories. The second level could be used for offices or apartments—or both.

I was excited about the land flanking either side of the place. The future was wide open.

I danced around Levi's spacious kitchen. He was in the shower. I glanced at the time. Ten more minutes were left on the cherry chocolate brownies in the oven. A good time to chat with Gran. She wasn't one to get tied down with phone conversations.

She picked up after two rings. "Briony—you waited long enough."

"I sent messages."

"They were like Dear Diary entries."

"We're in Silver Lake today. We're staying in Jade Hills another night."

"A grandmother needs more, especially after you say you're going to Peridot Falls."

"Sorry. I didn't mean to leave you hanging. I'm fine.

Levi's fine. I'm staying with him and... we're getting mated."

"Of course you are." Her tone was no nonsense. "You're a smart girl and you realized what a catch he is."

"He is a good catch."

"And you are too. He could tell right away."

I stuffed my stockinged foot into the floor, following the seam of the hardwood plank. "I thought I'd be nothing but problems, but the town is really open to me."

"It's the dragons. They can't go off like us. Don't be a pussy and they'll be fine with you."

I'd rather live in a community where I could also be weak and vulnerable, but shifters didn't see the world that way. At least the dragon shifters seemed to evaluate more of a personality than physical brutality.

"When's the big day?" she asked.

"I don't know. We just decided."

"Briony, that boy decided when he saw you. The date is up to you. The question is how long you want to make him wait—or maybe the real thing to ask is why."

I continued running my toe along the seam. Smooth wood traveled under my foot. I should set the date, but I should also come clean with Levi. He hadn't pressed me, and he wouldn't judge me. If anything, he'd be uncertain why I acted the way I did. And maybe those were the questions I hadn't wanted to face.

I should face them now. What I'd done was a turning point in my life. It'd changed me, and I wasn't sure it was for the better.

"Gran, there are some things I need to talk to you about. But I need to talk to Levi first."

"You've never been one to mince words, but I've always gotten a feeling you don't tell me everything. And your gentle father won't push you."

Father wasn't gentle, he was smart. He didn't want a battle between my family and another powerful family in the pack. It'd needlessly kill shifters and might've exposed us.

"I needed to come into my own. After what happened with Mom, I was… confused, for lack of a better term."

"Our world can be hard to figure out, even for our own kind." Gran's tone was surprisingly understanding.

I frowned. I should've gone to her earlier. But she'd been this formidable character—the leader of a mountain-lion-shifter pack—my entire life. She'd been as intimidating as she'd been loving.

"So, anyway, how have things been there?" I'd been gone a little over a week, but it felt more like two months. I wasn't the same Briony who'd left.

"It's quiet. Almost suspiciously."

Prickles spread across my body. "How so?"

"DJ's been lying low, but I went out last night. I'd already been for a walk and ran the pack meeting—and he and his sister are gone."

Dread dripped into my veins. "Ree too?"

"Yep."

It was an eight-hour drive here. No, they couldn't be coming to Peridot Falls. I'd moved on. This was a dragon-shifter community.

"Watch yourself, Bri," Gran said.

"Sure. I mean, they have better things to do than—"

"Briony. Levi rebuffed DJ and Ree blames you and your father for her missing aunt."

"Then her aunt shouldn't have killed my mother," I growled. I shook my head. I'd face all that soon enough. "Do you really think they left Canada to find me?"

"I wouldn't put it past them. I can't believe they'd be stupid enough to march into dragon-shifter territory to get to you, but there are valid ways. If they challenge you in Peridot Falls, I can't help."

Neither could Levi. Any interference on his part would diminish my credibility. The progress I made would be obliterated.

I hung up the phone, a sense of foreboding descending over me. The oven beeped, but I continued staring at the floor. I didn't believe in coincidences, and the shifters that had been the bane of my existence going suddenly radio silent was too suspicious.

Levi entered the kitchen on a chocolaty wave of amber. He stopped next to me, ducking his head down to meet my gaze, but I continued staring at the floor.

Another warning beep from the oven rang out. He left my side to switch the timer off and take out the batch of bars. Then he returned to stand next to me. "What's wrong?"

"I talked to Gran." Before I could say more, his phone started to ring.

He was going to ignore whoever was calling, but I shook my head. "Go ahead and answer." I had a feeling I couldn't shake, and the last time I'd felt this way was the day Mom was killed.

An image ran through my mind. Dad setting his phone on the countertop, his expression heavy, and his dark eyes full of concern. Mom hadn't returned from a night run. Gran hadn't heard from her and he had a sense of loss, impending grief he was afraid to explain. I'd run out the door and I'd found her. And then I'd hunted her killer.

Levi grabbed his phone from his pocket, his worried gaze on me.

"Answer it," I said.

A furrow developed between his brows but he did as I

asked. He didn't even get his hello out before Memphis's voice cut through.

"You and Briony need to get to my office. You have visitors."

Shit. I knew exactly who was at Memphis's door.

"Visitors?" Realization smoothed the creases from Levi's forehead. He might not know the details, but he'd figured out that whatever was bothering me was exactly what Memphis had called about. "What's going on?" His tone was even, but serious. A demand for an answer.

Memphis's reply was loud and clear. "Your mate is getting challenged."

CHAPTER 11

riony

Levi pulled up in front of city hall. I had expected the short Main Street to be empty, and it was—of cars. People were gathering along the sidewalks, and all the vehicles had been cleared out of the roadways as if they were expecting a parade. But there'd be no floats going down the street today. I had been issued a challenge I couldn't get out of.

And for once, I didn't want to.

Fed up and sick of the bullshit from the three cat shifters lingering outside the arched wooden door of city hall, I got out of the car and slammed the door behind me.

I recognized Jackie and Shelby in the crowd. Honor stood outside the café with her arms crossed. Their expressions were curious but also concerned. For me?

DJ stepped off the sidewalk and swaggered into the middle of the street.

I marched to him and shoved my finger into his shoulder, harder than he expected. An oomph left him as he struggled not to stagger back a step.

Satisfaction filtered through the haze of anger. He hadn't expected me to actually be strong. "I have no business with you." I didn't intend a shout but my volume was on high thanks to the emotions tumbling through me.

The corner of DJ's mouth kicked into an arrogant sneer. "Oh, but I'm not the one here to challenge you."

Sasha and Ree stepped onto the street and swaggered toward us like they had all the time in the world. But if I had my way, I'd cut their window on the face of the earth short. They terrorized enough people in Cougarton, and they'd hurt my gran when they were done with me. It was time for them to pay.

But other than being mean spirited and just plain selfish, I had to know what their purpose was. "Why? Why the hell couldn't you leave well enough alone? I was probably never going to go back to Cougarton, yet here you are."

Sasha's upper lip curled like she was going to bare a fang. "You don't deserve to get a free pass. These dragon shifters deserve to see you for the weak shifter you are."

Ree nodded, her dark eyes full of hate. "If it wasn't for your grandmother, you would've been taken care of long ago. Shifters like you shouldn't be allowed to exist." Her gaze darted to Levi. I didn't turn to look at him, but he must be hanging out by his car. "You shouldn't be allowed to come here and procreate and weaken the bloodline of our strongest shifters."

On the outside, her strategy was a good one. Ree wasn't blatantly insulting me. She was appealing to the pride of everyone around us, decreasing my perceived support from the others.

"You have no idea how weak or strong I am." I raised my voice for the next part. "You never came to my door and issued an official challenge. Other than DJ's attempt at the grocery store, you never faced me in public and said 'I challenge you.' You were content to hint and insinuate and let it get back to my gran. You hoped you'd face an older female instead of me—because no matter what, I'm a wild card." I started pacing, my adrenaline burning too much fuel in my veins for me to stand still. "You think you know me but you don't, and you all were too much of a coward to face me."

Sasha's face burned red, rage etched into the lines around her mouth. "Yeah? Then what are we doing here?"

As if I hadn't had time to put together my own assumptions about their motivations. "Because you think it's confirmation that I am hiding behind the dragon shifters, that I can't defend myself." I waved my fingers in a come-get-me move. "So come on. Let's find out."

Ree snorted. "You think you can take both of us at once?"

"What? Like it's hard?"

Rage was a mushroom cloud around them. The females ripped off their shirts over their heads. The first phase of this fight was a game of who could strip the fastest. Shifting later than your opponents would be a detriment. Grateful I didn't wear the jeweled jeans and tight-fitting tops they did, I kicked off my sandals and tugged my top over my head. The stakes were too high to care about being naked in a town full of strangers.

I was a cat shifter, and for once, I was embracing all that entailed.

I had to hand it to them, they were used to undressing and shifting far more frequently than I was. My shorts weren't over my hips and I was going to lose this race and get jumped by two mountain lions before I could even get my bra off.

"Maybe when this is over," I said, keeping a taunting gaze on Ree, knowing what I was about to say would cause her to go nuclear. "If you ask real nice, I'll tell you where I buried your aunt's body."

Her gasp echoed between the buildings. Her knees were bent, and she was crouched and ready to shift. But she froze, her wide eyes on me. "What did you do?"

My answer came out as a snarl. "I mercilessly killed her for what she did to my mom. Then I buried her where no one could find her because she didn't deserve mourning or a funeral for what she did."

Sasha's expression was pure disbelief. "Why wouldn't you tell anyone?"

My confession bought me time. "Because it would've only meant more death. I wanted the fighting to stop." My shorts hit the ground and I stepped out of them. "And it almost worked, but I underestimated just how nasty your families are. One death will never be enough for you."

I started to shift. DJ backed up a step, like he no longer wanted anything to do with this challenge. The females launched themselves at me before their shift had been completed.

A fire burned through my blood, a burn so hot, so unreal, it turned me into nothing but a beast of instinct. This had only happened once before, and I'd naively thought that it would be the last time.

But today, I embraced the sensation. I was facing two shifters who had wanted to get to my grandmother through me. They would continue to hurt others in their ever-widening search for power if I didn't put a stop to it.

I was no longer a young kid. I was a full adult, and it was time I dealt with this problem.

Snarls and high-pitched cat yells ripped through the air. I was oblivious to everyone and everything other than the two females I was fighting.

Was it a fair fight? Absolutely not. I could easily die, and this was the first time I wished I had more experience. I couldn't discount the pent-up rage from the last decade. These two hadn't been much older than me, but instead of using a loved one's disappearance to make their lives and the lives of others better, they terrorized those around them.

Teeth and claws bit into my hide and the metallic tang filled my mouth. Using my hind legs, I rabbit-punched Sasha off me while scrambling with Ree to get a good hold on her neck.

Ree was unprepared for the explosion of fury and energy, and she miscalculated. I slammed her to the ground and pounced on her, clamping my jaws around her neck. A strangled snarl cut off.

Sasha landed on my back but I was whipping my head back and forth too ferociously for her to gain purchase with her teeth. Bones crunched between my jaws and blood welled into my mouth. I didn't care if I killed Ree by bleeding her out or breaking her neck so completely she could never heal. The outcome would be the same.

Agony banged at the edge of my consciousness. Sasha was terrified for her friend and tried to get me to stop, but I was too strong for her. Or too stubborn, but either way, she couldn't get me to budge.

Ree went limp. I disengaged my jaws from around her neck and swung my head around to face her. Blood dripped from my mouth as I glared at her, challenging her to finish what she'd started.

My gaze said *one down, one more to go.*

Her fangs were bared but fear shook her body. She

realized she'd horribly underestimated me and she'd gone too far with the challenge to back out now. But I gave her time to think about it. If she wanted to bow out of this fight, I would let her. I had never wanted to hurt anyone, and after what happened the day my mother was murdered, I never wanted to be in another fight. This mindless peace terrified me as much as anyone else, but the pause gave me clarity.

I wasn't the same as the female who had murdered my mother. No longer would I be afraid to take on conflict. Others had suffered because I'd been too scared to admit what I'd done. Too scared the rest of my family wouldn't survive the resulting challenges. It had cost me a life, and it'd nearly cost me a mate.

But I wasn't an unthinking creature. The challenge had been issued. Ree was dying or already dead. If Sasha wanted to keep going, I'd take her on. But she had to make the choice. I might not be the same girl, but I wasn't running headfirst into violence just to prove myself.

The decision traveled over her like a storm cloud, her trembling decreasing as her muscles tightened. Determination to see this fight through was written across her body. And she attacked.

The fight was both easier and more difficult. I was only facing one big cat, but she had seen just how well I could defend myself. She rushed me, and I flung her off and paced, prepping for another attack.

DJ's voice cut between us. "Sasha, don't." His sister continued, "Stop." Out of the corner of my eye, I saw him approach.

"Don't interfere," came Levi's warning.

"She's going to kill her!" DJ shouted.

"As is the way of our people," Levi said. "You know that. You came to end Briony."

"Stay out of it, fucker. This would've never happened if you hadn't barged into town and taken her from me."

Sasha and I circled each other as DJ and Levi argued. I willed her to give up the fight, but deep down, I knew. Only one of us would be standing at the end.

Silver glinted in the sunlight, distracting me from the advancing cat. DJ had yanked a knife out of his pants leg and charged me. His sister chose that moment to attack.

Both were threats, but I chose to concentrate my efforts on Sasha. She was one of the two who had challenged me. She was who my fight was with. But as I rolled and clawed her, DJ's attack never came. There was a scuffle off to the side. Levi had tackled DJ, and they were wrestling over the knife. Gratitude swept through me and instead of diminishing my focus, it emboldened me. He had my back and the only people standing in the way of our happiness were the two shifters we were fighting.

I flipped around to Sasha's back and clamped my jaws around her neck. She screamed and tried to roll with me, but her strength was weakening. She wasn't used to fighting this length of time, and she was likely worried about her brother. Before sympathy could stop me from doing what needed to be done, I clenched my jaws and whipped my head side to side. Bone snapped between my teeth and her body went limp. I immediately released her. It was done.

I swung my head to search for Levi and found him standing over a prone DJ. A knife handle glinted between his ribs but a widening pool of blood indicated a more serious injury around his neck. A wound he wouldn't be able to heal from. I lurched to my side, my vision going hazy. The soft splatter of blood hitting the ground made me look down. Did I have that much of Sasha and Ree's blood on me? I tried to take a step, and it was like someone had let all the air out of me. I folded onto the ground.

Levi rushed to my side and buried his hands into my fur, the action causing as much pain as the pleasure of his touch. "Hang in there, Briony. You need to rest so you can heal."

I tried to nod, but my eyes were droopy and I let out a sigh. It was done. Years of hiding a secret, unsure whether I was doing the right thing, fearing for my family had exhausted me.

I closed my eyes and concentrated on Levi's presence. Hoping I had enough energy to heal and wake up to him again.

~

Levi

I PUT my arm around my new mate and faced the crowd filled with our friends and family. We were standing outside the building we had converted into a bakery. "Thanks for coming, everyone. Since these two parts of our lives are so intimately entwined—"

"You're fucking in the bakery?" Maverick's voice rang out.

The crowd snickered, and I chuckled. "You have our utmost assurances that if we did fuck in the bakery, we would use the best hygienic practices possible."

Briony elbowed my side, failing to hold back a grin. Her cheeks were dusted with pink, but she handled her embarrassment like a pro. "We love each other as much as we love running a business together," she said to the crowd, "so it made sense to have the party in the bakery after the ceremony."

I was no longer a single male. Truth be told, I'd been taken as soon as I'd laid my eyes on her. And since I'd gobbled that first batch of chocolate cherry bars, it had seemed like destiny had carried us to this point. As soon as she woke up healed, a full twenty-four hours after she'd faced Sasha and Ree, she announced that we should mate as soon as possible, that she didn't want to hold back in her life anymore.

The town had liked her before, but after the showdown in the middle of the street, and her confession of how she'd handled her mother's death, she was a revered member of the community. She'd been scared of her grandmother's reaction and what others would think, but she'd been a kid. A kid who'd avenged her mom's death and then protected her family and the pack. No one faulted her. Townsfolk were damn proud she was a part of Peridot clan.

But none of how they felt came near the emotions coursing through me right now. My brother and Memphis were grinning at us. Venus had stayed in Jade Hills so Lachlan and Indy could come to the ceremony. And since Venus was in Jade Hills, Penn said he'd watch over Silver Lake so Deacon and Steel could attend our mating ceremony.

Without DJ, Sasha, and Ree, Enid hadn't worried about leaving Cougarton to travel here. Briony's uncle Lewis sent his best wishes. Enid had been staying with us for three days, working just as hard on the bakery to get it ready for the reception as we had been. Yesterday, Briony had spent her day in the kitchen baking our wedding cake—chocolate cherry flavored—and assembling appetizers for our guests.

Gran's Sweets wouldn't open for another few weeks,

but the place was ready enough to host the gathering. The apartments above the bakery would be finished shortly after, and then Briony and I would figure out what we wanted to do with the land flanking either side.

She'd already hired a couple of teenagers to run the till and a shifter from Opal's clan had stopped in to inquire about a baker position. Briony hadn't considered turning over the job to anyone but her, but we were also going to be running other businesses and it would be handy to have her freed up. Neither of us could believe how fast we were growing and the level of interest we garnered.

"And now," I announced, "for the unofficial grand opening of Gran's Sweets."

I swung the doors open and everyone piled past us, shaking hands, giving out hugs, and patting us on the back.

Briony's father stepped in to give her a solid kiss on the forehead and slapped me on the back with a meaty fist. I hadn't seen him before the big fight, but Enid had mentioned he looked a solid decade younger than the last time she'd seen them. Briony hadn't been the only one carrying the weight of their secret. But in addition to the burden of what had happened to his wife and her attacker, he'd had to shoulder the worry of how it affected his daughter. He'd even mentioned moving closer to us now that his inner turmoil had subsided. In fact, he would be one of our first tenants in the apartment, happy to give up farming and sell his property and spoil grandchildren. Those were his words.

The kids would come eventually, but until then, I was thoroughly going to enjoy my new mate and the life we were building together.

Everyone was inside, and I faced Briony. "Ready to show everyone how well you can bake?"

She smirked. "I think some of them are going to be surprised they've already tasted my cinnamon rolls."

I laughed. "Facts."

She'd been making test batches for Honor to sell in the café, and in return, Honor had her paintings hanging in the bakery with a tiny price tag attached to each one.

I glanced into the building, watching everyone milling around. Her dad was eyeing the paintings on the wall. Enid was filling her plate with each type of appetizer—pinwheels, buffalo wings, and veggies. Memphis was laughing with Jackie and her mate while my brother was brooding out the far window.

The only shadow cast over the day. There was no more on-again, off-again relationship for him. That window faced the direction of the property his ex's new mate owned. The place wasn't visible, but it didn't matter. Maverick insisted on acting like nothing bothered him, but I could tell that my mating before him was unsettling.

I hoped he found someone. He couldn't put my sister in a position of punishing him.

Briony squeezed my hand. "Go talk to him. It's okay."

"It's our big day."

She gave me another reassuring squeeze. "A day that would be nothing without everyone in this place. Go talk to him."

I did as she said, coming to a stop next to him at the window. I shoved my hands in the pockets of my slacks and gazed out the glass at the line of trees. "I know it sucks, man."

"Yeah." Except for the day we'd had the talk in Deacon's kitchen, he hadn't said much about the matter. He spun around and put his back to the window. "I'm going to have to leave soon and I hope you don't take it personally."

"Where are you going?" We hadn't had much time to

talk about non-work-related subjects since I'd returned to town, but I wasn't prepared to hear he was ditching me.

As if he sensed the direction of my thoughts, he said, "Don't take it personally. I need to get away from everything. Shifters included."

If I hadn't met Briony, I'd have a harder time understanding. But thanks to her, I could see how our way of life and the rules and traditions we were required to abide by could change. They could be isolating and suffocating. "Where are you going?"

"Vegas. No place like the city of sin to get your mind off things."

Surprise ricocheted through me. I thought maybe he'd go to Minneapolis, or even Duluth. Somewhere in the state. But Vegas? "I'd tell you to stay out of trouble, but maybe that's what you need."

He cracked a smile, but it didn't reach his eyes. "You never know." He clapped me on the back, and just like that, I sensed the subject was closed. "Oh, hey, I need to get some pinwheels before Memphis takes them all."

He wandered away, and I stayed where I was for a moment, trying to encapsulate the worry for my brother.

Briony's cinnamon-sugar smell washed over me. "That didn't go well?" she asked as she wrapped her arms around my waist.

"He's going to Vegas," I murmured.

Her brows lifted, and she slid her gaze to watch Maverick muscle his way through the buffet line. "Maybe he'll come home with a wife."

I snorted out a laugh. "I thought maybe getting into trouble could be just what he needed, but none of us need those kinds of problems."

"It worked for you."

"No—" Wait. I thought about everything that brought

me to her. If I hadn't unknowingly fucked up, I never would've met my mate. "I guess it did. We'll have to wait and see if he's as lucky of a bastard as I am."

"Until then…" She rose onto her tiptoes to whisper in my ear. "I made a special batch of cherry chocolate bars that you can eat—after I place them strategically all over my body."

A groan left me. "The storeroom in the back is empty."

She giggled. "Not for long."

This was the best day of my life and it was only going to get better.

———

FIND out if Maverick comes home with a wife—and if she'll become his mate in The Dragon's Dedication.

FOR NEW RELEASE UPDATES, chapter sneak peeks, and exclusive quarterly short stories, sign up for Marie's newsletter and receive my first wolf shifter story FREE.

THANK YOU FOR READING. I'd love to know what you thought. Please consider leaving a review for The Dragon's Word at the retailer the book was purchased from.

ABOUT THE AUTHOR

Marie Johnston writes paranormal and contemporary romance and has collected several awards in both genres. Before she was a writer, she was a microbiologist. Depending on the situation, she can be oddly unconcerned about germs or weirdly phobic. She's also a licensed medical technician and has worked as a public health microbiologist and as a lab tech in hospital and clinic labs. Marie's been a volunteer EMT, a college instructor, a security guard, a phlebotomist, a hotel clerk, and a coffee pourer in a bingo hall. All fodder for a writer!! She has four kids, an old cat, and a puppy that's bigger than half her kids.

mariejohnstonwriter.com

Follow me:

ALSO BY MARIE JOHNSTON

Silver Dragon Shifter Brothers

The Dragon's Oath

The Dragon's Promise

The Dragon's Vow

Jade Dragon Shifter Brothers

The Dragon's Pledge

The Dragon's Bond

Peridot Dragon Shifter Brothers

The Dragon's Word

The Dragon's Dedication

The Dragon's Affirmation

Printed in Great Britain
by Amazon

23661949R00108